HOLIDA

A Killer Coffee Mystery

Book Seven

BY
TONYA KAPPES

TONYA KAPPES
WEEKLY NEWSLETTER

Want a behind-the-scenes journey of me as a writer?
The ups and downs, new deals, book sales, giveaways and more? I share it all! Join the exclusive Southern Sleuths private group today! Go to www.patreon.com/Tonyakappesbooks

As a special thank you for joining, you'll get an exclusive copy of my cross-over short story, *A CHARMING BLEND.* Go to Tonyakappes.com and click on subscribe at the top of the home page.

ACKNOWLEDGMENTS

Thank you to the amazing readers who send in recipes to be included in the Killer Coffee Series.

Burnt Sugar Cake was submitted by Jeannie Daniel, Twinkie Cake was submitted by Robin Kyle, and Rich Potato Chowder was submitted by Chris Mayer. I've made all of them, and they are amazing! I hope you try them too. Be sure to let me know if you do!

I'd also like to thank Mariah Sinclair for the adorable covers for the Killer Coffee Mystery Series. They are so fun and Pepper makes the cover.

Thank you to Red Adept Editing for the wonderful editing job you do to make my words make sense.

And a huge thank you to my husband Eddy. He does all the things that would normally take me away from writing. Without him by my side, I'd not be able to be a full-time writer and fulfill my dream.

CHAPTER ONE

The twinkling Christmas lights that wrapped around the wooded deck of the Watershed Restaurant added a shimmer atop Lake Honey Springs. A nice romantic evening with Patrick was exactly what I needed to get into the spirit of the season.

Since I'd been working so many long holiday hours at the Bean Hive, my coffee shop, I'd been busy getting all the holiday coffee blends and special-ordered baked sweet treats ready for my customers, so I'd not taken much time for my relationship with my husband or our fur babies, Pepper and Sassy.

"You look beautiful." Patrick Cane reached over and laid his hand on mine.

Patrick's big brown eyes, tender smile, and sensitive heart drew me into him when we were just teenagers and I came to Honey Springs during the summers to visit my aunt. "I'm glad we made time for me and you."

"Me too." I put my other hand on top of his and rubbed it. I couldn't stop blushing. My heart skipped a beat.

Patrick owned Cane Construction, and the economy had been booming around our small town of Honey Springs, Kentucky, so he was just as busy as I had been at the coffee shop.

Neither of us were complaining because we certainly had seasons of dry spells in which the money just trickled in.

"Geez, buddy!" A man sitting next to us jumped up when the busboy accidentally knocked his table and spilled the man's water in his lap. "Watch what you're doing."

"Calm down, Ryan." The woman across from him had turned red, though she was trying to hide her face behind her blonde hair. She looked around the restaurant to see if anyone was watching.

Of course everyone could hear them. They were louder than the jazz band playing Christmas carols in the corner of the restaurant.

"Are you joking?" Ryan glared over at her and he quickly replaced the man's glass with another glass of water and apologized before hurrying away.

"No, I'm not joking," she spat. "You can be such a jerk. Things happen."

The man grabbed the glass and took a drink, glaring at the woman across from him before he went back to finishing his meal.

"That looks delicious." Patrick and I pulled back our hands so Fiona Rosone, our waitress, could put our plates on the table, taking the attention off the couple next to us.

Patrick's loving gaze had turned from me to the honey-glazed salmon on his plate.

I had ordered the panko-encrusted chicken, one of the Watershed's specials, along with a plain sweet potato and asparagus. I would definitely take some of the sweet potato home with me to give to Sassy and Pepper. Not only did they love it, but sweet potato was good for their digestion and their coats.

On most days, the dogs came to work with me, and I tried to keep an eye on them so customers wouldn't slip them something they'd ordered from the counter, but it was hard to police that. Plus, Pepper was a wonderful vacuum and sniffed out any little morsel of food.

"The babies?" Patrick's smile lit up his face when he noticed I was saving some of my food.

"Of course." I shrugged, knowing how much I treated them like real human babies. Having children was something Patrick and I did want, but it wasn't in the foreseeable future.

We'd only been married a year after many years apart, during which time I'd gone to college, attended law school, started a law firm with my now-ex-husband, and then moved here to open the Bean Hive. It took all that time to find the life I considered to be... well... perfect.

"It's so pretty here tonight." I looked out the window of the floating restaurant.

Logsdon Landscaping had done a fantastic job decorating. The Christmas tree on the outside deck glowed with colored lights and fun lake-themed ornaments. The Christmas trees inside the Watershed were decorated a little more elegantly, with white lights and fancy ornaments with glitter, large ribbons, and bows. Beside the tree outside sat a sign on a fancy gold stand declaring Logsdon Landscaping Co. the decorator.

Amy Logsdon had taken over the dying family landscaping business. When she did, she saw a need for people's help in decorating for all the seasons because we celebrated and decorated every holiday on the calendar. We'd even had our annual Christmas festival in the town square last weekend.

The Pawrade was still my favorite event of the entire festival. In the Pawrade, we dressed up our fur babies and raised money for the local Pet Palace, Honey Springs's local SPCA.

But what Amy did to turn the company around was amazing. She took the landscaping business to a whole other level. She took clients, like the Watershed, and completely decorated the exteriors and interiors of the buildings in addition to storing the decorations all year long instead of having the business try to find a place to store them. This part of Logsdon Landscaping focused primarily on the outside decorations. Some people had hired the company to come to their homes and put up their lights, their large yard displays, and more.

It really did help cut back on all the work the Beautification Committee had to do, freeing up their time to focus more on the business side of the festivals.

Focusing on that was a very nice option to have, but I loved to decorate and had made it part of my life, which helped me get so excited for the holidays.

"It is pretty." Patrick looked over the candlelight at me. "You make it prettier."

"We are already married. You can stop laying it on thick." I couldn't stop smiling.

Fiona knew us so well, she'd already brought a to-go box over to the table. She knew I needed the box so I could take home the dogs' portion.

"That was so good." Patrick pulled his wallet out of his pocket, took out the cash for the bill, and leaned back in his chair. "Now we can go home, snuggle with the kids by the fire for a few minutes before we decorate our tree."

"Heaven." Sometimes I couldn't believe I'd hit the jackpot in my thirties. In my twenties, it was a bumpy ride but worth every up and down it took to get to this moment right here. Plus, Patrick was such a romantic. He loved cutting down a live tree and decorating it. He had a full night planned, and I would definitely go along with it.

We smiled at each other before the couple next to us interrupted with their loud argument.

"I told you that I've had it." The woman pointed at the man with her steak knife. "I won't put up with this behavior anymore."

"Keep your voice down," the man shushed her. "When we got married, you knew exactly what you were getting into."

"I've had enough." She picked her napkin up from her lap and wiped her mouth. "After Christmas, I'm filing for divorce."

"Over my dead body." He threw his napkin on his plate.

"So be it." She slammed her napkin on the table, and water splashed out of her glass.

The scooting sounds of their chairs did cause others to look around, but since they were next to me and Patrick, I think we were the only ones who heard them arguing.

Patrick and I watched the couple rush out of the restaurant.

"I hope we don't ever get like that when we reach their age." Their sadness gnawed in my gut, and I couldn't help but wonder if they were once all goo-goo eyed like Patrick and I were.

"Never. Ever." He shook his head. "Unless Penny and Maxi stop getting along… then we might have a problem," he said, joking about the sudden friendship between my mom and aunt.

"I wouldn't be joking about them because they've already had a falling out this week about who was going to bring the fruitcake on Christmas." I let out a long sigh.

"You decide." Patrick thought it was as easy as that when it clearly wasn't.

You see, my mom, Penny Bloom, and my aunt Maxine Bloom had never gotten along in my entire life, until recently. My mom had been really jealous of my relationship with my aunt Maxi. And well… let's just say that I've always had a connection with my Aunt Maxi I'd never had with my mom, and when I got divorced, it was of course Aunt Maxi I'd run to. Here I was a few years later with some history under my belt, and my mom had moved to Honey Springs. She and Aunt Maxi were the reason Patrick and I were married by the justice of the peace.

"I've got enough people to coordinate without refereeing them." I was now rethinking my decision to host a big Christmas Day supper for my friends and family at the Bean Hive Coffee Shop.

My friends had become family in our small community, and I wanted them to surround me during the holidays. Everyone had something special to bring to the occasion, which would be a joyous one even if Mom and Aunt Maxi decided not to get along.

"Will that be all?" Fiona asked and picked up the check with the cash.

"Yes. Very good." Patrick leaned back and patted his stomach. "Keep the change."

"Delicious as always." It was a treat to come to the Watershed, and it took some effort to actually get dressed, put on makeup, and look presentable. Not like when I went to work at the coffee shop with my hair pulled up and my baking clothes on underneath my Bean Hive apron.

Patrick, being the southern gentleman he was, got up from his chair and walked over to help me out of mine.

"Let's get home and decorate our own tree." Patrick reached his hand out to me.

"Fire, snuggles, decorating." I took his hand in mine. "Patrick Cane, you are something else."

"I just want to keep you happy during this Christmas get-together." We walked toward the back of the restaurant so we could go outside to look at the decorations. "I know how stressed you can get, and if I can help out, I'm going to. So you"—he opened the door to the outside and had me walk past him—"my dear, will be pampered by me."

He pulled me to him once the door shut behind us and shielded me from the winter night wind, which whipped across the lake and over us, sending chills along my body.

Patrick stood behind me with his arms wrapped around me, and we looked across the lake to the Bee Farm, where Kayla and Andrew Noro had put up a big display of wood cutouts of bees wearing Santa hats. The display was all lit up so the people on the land side of the lake could see and enjoy it.

The Bee Farm was a small island in the middle of the lake. It was amazing to visit and see exactly how the bee farm worked. I got all my honey from Kayla. It was so fresh and tasty, not only in the coffees and teas I served at The Bean Hive but also in the baked goods.

"Everyone seems to be really ready for this season compared to last year." Patrick's warm breath tickled my ear. He rested his chin on my shoulder.

"Why did you mention that?" I jerked around and looked at him. "You are giving us bad juju."

Last year, a murder took place during the Pawrade at the annual Christmas tree lighting in Central Park, located in downtown Honey Springs. I wanted to forget that forever.

"It's not bad juju." He laughed and grabbed my hand. "Let's get home to the kids."

We were walking along the Watershed's pier toward the parking lot when we heard the same couple from inside the restaurant arguing outside near their truck.

"I'm telling you that I'm not going to stand for this. Do you understand?" Ryan yelled at the woman, who I assumed was his wife since he'd said something about how she knew before they got married this was how it was.

"You know what?" The woman jerked the door open. "I'm going to call a lawyer!"

The couple both slammed their doors. The tires squealed as their truck took off.

Patrick's grip tightened on my hand.

"I think that's Ryan Moore's truck." Patrick seemed to recognize people's vehicles more than their faces. "He owns the butcher shop where I pick up those steaks and chops you like so much."

"They seem very unhappy." I frowned.

"I don't think they are going to have a good Christmas." He opened the passenger-side door for me.

"Don't worry." I kissed him before I got in. "It took me a divorce to find you. I'm for sure not going to let you go."

I hooked my seatbelt while he got inside the truck.

The Watershed was on one far left side of the boardwalk, which held many specialty shops along with the Bean Hive.

My coffee shop had a perfect location right in the middle of all the shops. Directly in front of the coffee shop was a long pier that jutted out and was perfect for people who liked to fish deeper out into the water.

"I love how they put the lighted garland around all the carriage posts," Patrick said about all the lights along the boardwalk. "It's prettier than just the wreaths the committee has put up in past years."

"Yes, but the Beautification Committee did the best they could with what they had." I still had to give Loretta Bebe credit. She did work hard on trying to make Honey Springs gorgeous during the festive times of the year.

Our cabin was located about a seven-minute drive from the boardwalk, which was a very windy road running along the lake. I usually rode my bike with Pepper nestled in the front basket while Sassy went to work with Patrick at the construction sites for most of the day until he stopped in for a cup of coffee. That was when she liked to stay at the coffee shop with Pepper and me.

Lately, it was either too cold or there was too much ice on the road to ride the bike.

"Be careful," I warned Patrick when he took one of the sharper curves. "The weather report said there could be some black ice on the road."

The taillights of Ryan Moore's truck showed the vehicle had started to cross over the center line of the small road.

"There must be some up there." Patrick pointed at the car. We watched as the driver jerked the truck back over. "Whoa!"

"Oh no!" I yelled as we watched the truck cross over again, this time going through the trees and down the embankment toward the lake.

I eased up in the seat of Patrick's truck and looked down to see if the people in the truck were okay when we got to the place they'd gone off the road.

"Call 911!" Patrick yelled at me. He put his truck in park when we saw the other truck had actually gone into Lake Honey Springs, with the front end heading underwater.

I fumbled for my phone and dialed while trying to see Patrick through the pitch dark of night. The headlights of the sunken truck were fading fast into the depths of the water.

I rattled off the information to the dispatch operator and jumped out of the car when I saw Patrick had jumped into the lake. I grabbed the blankets and his work flashlight out from behind the seat and headed down to the lake.

"Patrick!" I screamed when I didn't see him come back up. "Patrick!"

I frantically screamed, dropping the blankets on the beach and shining the flashlight in the water. "Patrick!"

I ran up and down where the truck had gone in, but I was not sure where it was because I could no longer see the headlights. When I heard some splashing a few yards out in the lake, I moved the flashlight and saw Patrick.

"I've got the woman!" Patrick swam toward the bank with the woman in the crock of his arm. She was coughing and wheezing. "She's alive!"

In the distance, I could hear the sirens. They echoed off the lake. I ran to meet Patrick and the woman, holding one of the blankets to wrap around her.

"I've got to go and get Mr. Moore." He laid her gently on her side on the ground before he went right back into the water.

"Here," I told her, picking up more blankets and then wrapping them around her. "Are you okay?" I asked.

She looked up at me.

"My husband," she tried to say but was shivering. "My husband!" She jumped up as the shock of it all started to set in. "Ryan!" she screamed.

"Please, put this around you until the ambulance gets here." I tried to put the blanket back on her shoulders, but she attempted to run back into the water. "Stop! Don't go back in there!"

"Ryan!" It was all she seemed to say while I jerked her back and literally held her back.

The ambulance and police showed up, taking over just as Patrick came back up from the depths of Lake Honey Springs with the limp man over his shoulder.

After Patrick got him to shore, we let the emergency crew take over.

"What happened?" Sheriff Spencer Shepard asked when he got there.

"I think they hit black ice because we saw them swerve, then correct, then swerve again, ending up in the lake," Patrick told Spencer while we stood to the side and watched the EMTs give Ryan CPR. "We saw them having supper at the Watershed. It's Ryan and Yvonne Moore. He owns the butcher shop in town."

"Yeah." Spencer's brows furrowed as he nodded.

The bright yellow lights of the tow truck circled, lighting up the darkness. The people in the tow truck were working on retrieving the Moores' truck from the depths of the lake while the emergency workers continued to attend to Ryan.

"No!" Yvonne fell to the ground, lying on Ryan and grabbing our attention.

Spencer excused himself and hurried over to see what was going on. We watched as the emergency workers looked at Spencer and shook their heads.

"Oh no." I gasped, bringing my hand up to my mouth, knowing Ryan Moore was dead.

CHAPTER TWO

I sprang into action and headed straight over to Yvonne Moore. Though I didn't know her, I knew this was not what was expected. Of course I'd heard them arguing, but who didn't argue? We said things all the time that we really didn't mean, and I was sure this was what'd happened between this couple.

Yvonne had refused medical treatment, and I sat with her, letting her talk to me. Mostly she just rambled. I was sure she was still in shock. Since owning the Bean Hive, I'd learned how to be a really great listener. People loved to talk over a nice big cup of joe. The liquid was better than truth serum.

"What am I going to do?" Yvonne's eyes frantically searched my face like I had her answer.

"We are going to call someone for you. But first, we are going to go sit in Patrick's truck. It's too cold out here." I guided her to the truck and tried to watch out for anything she could step on so it didn't hurt her bare feet. "We can use my phone. Who would you like to call?" Once I got her in the passenger side of the truck, I held out my phone.

She pushed it away.

"I have no one." She looked out the windshield, nervously picking at her fingernails. "My mom lives with us. But she's elderly. She doesn't drive, so she can't come..."

"I'm so sorry." I rubbed her back, hoping to give her at least a little comfort. I just couldn't imagine if I didn't have anyone, and that was what her case seemed to be. I remembered the small bag of clothes Patrick kept behind his seat for the times when he was working in the rain or snow. "Your feet must be freezing."

I reached around the back of the seat and pulled the duffle bag over. I flipped on the interior light and unzipped the bag to take out the socks.

"Here, put these on," I told her, and she took them from me.

"Thank you. I slipped off my heels in the truck after we got in and..." She shook her head. The tears continued to pour. "Ryan always made fun of me because I never wore anything but heels. I don't even own a pair of tennis shoes, and here we are in a lake town with some hiking and outdoor things."

I listened to her ramble. It must've felt good to get it out.

"I can't stand gardening or any sort of outside work, so when I'm in the house, I like to go barefooted." She smiled, but then her expression faded to a frown, and more tears fell down her cheeks. "Ryan said he loved that about me, how I always kept myself always pristine. He had no problem hiring landscapers."

"Do you have any children?" I asked, hoping to figure out who I could call for her, though she said she had no one.

"No." She shook her head. "Just my mom."

We sat there in the dark, silent truck as we watched the workers take Ryan's body and put it into the hearse.

Spencer walked over and knocked on my window.

"Ma'am, I'm sorry about your husband." He was good at comforting people during times of loss. "I'm going to need to ask you a few questions if that's okay."

"Yes. Sure. Anything." Yvonne nodded.

"Can you tell me if you'd been drinking?" Spencer asked.

"No. We had left the Watershed and were driving home." She

continued to shake her head and blink as though she were trying to remember something. "We had water, but while he was driving, I noticed he'd begun to slur his speech. He'd started shaking and gone over the line in the road when I asked him if he was okay. That's when it went from bad to worse. The truck veered off the road, and the next thing I remember is being pulled out of the water by that man." She pointed out the window at Patrick.

"Did your husband have any sort of medical condition?" Spencer was taking notes on his little notepad.

"No. He had his yearly physical back in October, and from what I recall, all the blood work came back normal and no other tests were scheduled." Yvonne wiped off a dripping tear. I reached over and patted her.

"What about drug use? Did your husband use recreational drugs?" His questioning made Yvonne jerk up. He'd definitely offended her.

"Absolutely not, and I will not let you say anything like that," she said immediately.

"I'm afraid there was a reason your husband drove off the road. If he was in good health, not drinking or doing any sort of recreational drugs, I'm going to have an autopsy done just so you'll know exactly what caused his death." Through Spencer's sly sheriff ways, I could tell he was trying to get her to agree to an autopsy. In the state of Kentucky, the law didn't ask for an autopsy unless they suspected foul play.

"Oh, okay." Yvonne shrugged. "Sure." She readily agreed.

If I was her lawyer, I'd tell her to take the night to think about the situation, but I wasn't, so I kept my lips sealed.

Not that I was still a practicing lawyer. I wasn't, but I did keep my credentials up and could practice if I wanted to. Still, although I never thought Yvonne did anything to her husband while they were in the car, I couldn't stop mentally replaying her and Ryan fighting not only in the Watershed but also in the parking lot. If I remembered correctly, there were a few "over my dead body" comments, and now he was dead. That was a red flag to me. Coincidence? Maybe.

Then it dawned on me. I bet Patrick told Spencer about the Moores' fight.

"Is there anyone we can call for you?" he asked, ending his questions because he was satisfied with her agreeing to the autopsy, which would answer any questions he might have.

"No one I can think of." She shivered.

"Patrick and I can take her home," I told Spencer. "She said her mother lives with her, so she won't be alone tonight."

"Is that all right, Mrs. Moore?" He looked through the truck at her.

"Yes. Of course." She eagerly nodded then looked at me with a pinched smile and grateful gleam in her eye before the sadness drew back over her.

Yvonne and I sat in silence as we waited for Patrick to finish talking to Spencer and the tow-truck driver. They'd yet to pull the truck out, but I really did think they were waiting until we took Yvonne home. It was something she probably shouldn't see.

"Mrs. Moore, I'm Patrick Cane. I guess you met my wife, Roxanne." He was so good about introductions when I'd never even told her my name.

"Roxy. You can call me Roxy," I told her, leaving out my usual, "my friends call me Roxy." I think this situation already called for us to be friends.

"I normally would say it's nice to meet you, but right now I really can't wrap my head around what's happened." She continued to stare out the window from the passenger side. I sat in between her and Patrick.

"You don't need to say anything." I continued to pat her. It was the only thing I knew to do to comfort her. Not that petting her like I did Pepper was any comfort, but I was at a loss here.

"If there's anything we can do for you, you just reach out to us." Again, Patrick always seemed to know the right things to say.

"Thank you. I guess they will let me know when they will release him so I can make arrangements." She started to sob all over again.

I just continued to pat her but glanced over at Patrick. The lights on the dashboard created enough light to see his eyes. They held sadness for Yvonne. We both felt it for her.

"I know where you live." Patrick took the winding road past our cabin and headed deeper into the wooded part of Honey Springs, where one found big farms and farmland. He was heading toward the Hill Orchard.

"Thank you," Yvonne whispered. She was trying to pull herself together. She shifted, sniffed, and tried to fix her hair, which had dried and left strands stuck to her face. "I just don't know what happened. One minute we were…" She stopped herself from talking, but I bet she was going to say "fussing." "It was like he just fell asleep. I bet it was a heart attack. Don't those take you pretty fast?"

"I have no medical knowledge." I wasn't going to say one thing or another. Fast or not fast, something happened to her husband. "The autopsy will bring the closure you need."

I wanted to say something about God's timing or things happening for a reason, but I didn't. I didn't think those words would make her feel any better, and getting her home to her mom was probably the best thing.

When Patrick pulled into the asphalt driveway that I'd driven by so many times and came up to the gate, I was a bit excited. While passing by this gate and driveway, I'd often wondered who lived there or what was back there.

"Can I help you?" A woman's voice came from the box on the post after Patrick pushed the button.

"Daryl, it's Yvonne. Please let us in." Before Yvonne got the entire sentence out, the gate started to open. "Please ignore the half Christmas lights. The company we hired won't have everything completed until the end of the week. Ryan loved Christmas and all the fanfare."

"Logsdon Landscaping?" I asked, though I already knew the answer because I'd seen their trucks pulling into the driveway when I'd driven past.

"Yes. I believe that's them. You use them?" she asked. "Ryan loves them. They do all our landscaping too."

"I don't use them, but I own a little coffee shop on the boardwalk, and they've done all the Christmas decorations for the Beautification Committee this year," I said and looked both ways going up the driveway.

I could see why Ryan had him do their landscaping. They had a lot of land. The massive red brick home was all lit up with spotlights, and the fountain in the circle drive didn't show any signs of freezing in the cold temperature as the carven swans spewed water.

"The Bean Hive?" Yvonne turned slightly and asked.

"Yes. You've been there?" I questioned.

"I have. Mostly at night when Ryan and I finish having dinner out..." Her voice trailed off again as if she'd just remembered what happened.

The house's door opened. Two women, one older and one younger, stood there.

Yvonne opened the door and got out. I slid over and followed her up to the door while Patrick stayed in the truck.

"Mom, Ryan..." Yvonne couldn't even finish her words before she collapsed.

"Yvonne!" The younger woman knelt and tried to help Yvonne.

Without even having to look, I heard Patrick's door slam and his footsteps racing up to help out.

"What is going on?" the old woman asked, tugging the shawl around her shoulders. Her hair was pulled up in a tight grey bun on the top of her head. "Who are you? Daryl, call the police."

Daryl was too busy trying to wake Yvonne up to so much as think about calling the police.

"Ma'am, I'm Patrick Cane, and this is my wife Roxanne. We saw your daughter and her husband's truck run off the road. Unfortunately, your son-in-law didn't make it. I did pull them both out of the water."

"Water? What do you mean didn't make it?" The older woman sounded as though she were searching for answers.

"If I can get Mrs. Moore inside, we will explain it all." He handed her a business card. "This is Sheriff Spencer Shepard's information. He asked me to give this to you since Mrs. Moore is not in any shape at this time to really comprehend what has happened to her and Mr. Moore."

"Get them in the house," Yvonne's mother said. Patrick picked up Yvonne, who regained consciousness, and Yvonne's mother gestured for Daryl to appear.

I'd like to say I was looking around at the house since this was my one chance, but I was so focused on poor Yvonne that I didn't even notice anything but the suede couch Patrick had laid her down on.

Daryl had come back with a tray of waters, giving Yvonne her own personal straw. We all sat down and watched Yvonne become increasingly aware. Patrick told her mom what had happened. He did leave out the part of us overhearing them argue, which was going to be our little secret.

Or so I thought.

CHAPTER THREE

Patrick and I stayed only about another half hour at the Moores' home. Yvonne had started recalling all the details, and we knew it was our time to leave. Both of us remained silent until we got home. I wasn't sure what Patrick was thinking, but I was thinking, *What if that was me?* and feeling really sad for Yvonne.

We had very little time for our previous plans of making a fire, doing a little decorating, and snuggling with the dogs after we got home. Instead we snuggled with the dogs in our bed. Patrick had no problem, as usual, going to sleep. I wasn't sure how he did it, but as soon as the covers were pulled up to his chin, he was out for the night, even after all the excitement we'd had.

I was a totally different story. So was Pepper. Pepper couldn't get situated. I couldn't get settled. Both of us just tossed and turned, taking a few sideways glances over at Sassy and Patrick, who were both out like lights.

"Okay," was all I had to whisper before Pepper jumped off the bed and I followed closely behind him.

Our home was a neat little cabin that I'd purchased when I moved to Honey Springs. Long story short, Patrick had ended up buying my Aunt Maxi's gorgeous home overlooking Lake Honey Springs. When we got married, one of the hardest decisions we had to make was where we were going to call home.

Of course, we both wanted to stay in our respective houses, and ultimately I won. The nice cozy feel of my cabin was perfect for the four of us. The cabin had a family-room-and-kitchen combo as you entered off the covered front porch, which, by the way, was across the street from the lake and had the most gorgeous view. Plus, the back side of the cabin was surrounded by the woods, making it very private. This time of the year, the leaves were already off the trees, and snow would arrive any day now, making the environment a beautiful winter wonderland.

The small kitchen was perfect for the cooking we did. So for this season of our life, the cabin was perfect. Plus, it was just a few minutes to get to the boardwalk.

There was no sense in waking up Patrick. He would know exactly where Pepper and I had gone when he woke up—the Bean Hive.

Since it was bitterly cold out and the morning sun had not even thought about waking up, I quickly got my things together, put Pepper's coat on him, put my own coat on, and headed out the door.

"It's gonna be a chilly one," I told Pepper on our way out. I fumbled with the keys to unlock the car door. Pepper eagerly jumped in the front seat. "We will have to keep the fire going all day."

Pepper wiggled around like he knew he was about to spend the day either on one of the coffee shop's couches or on his dog bed. Both were located in front of the fireplace. He was spoiled.

I couldn't help but slow way down when I passed the Moores' crash site. The torn-up ground where the tow truck had pulled Ryan Moore's truck out of the lake was still fresh.

Goosebumps crawled along my arm just thinking about what had taken place a few short hours ago. I gripped the wheel and made sure I took the curves super slow. Black ice was exactly that—ice on the road that was hard to detect because of the black asphalt. When your tires came into contact with black ice, you barely knew what hit you. I still couldn't help but wonder if the Moores had continued to argue in the truck and Ryan hadn't been paying full attention to the road when they slid. But I also remembered Yvonne saying Ryan had started to shake. Was it from anger? Then again, she was in shock, so I wasn't sure she knew what she was even talking about.

I pulled my car into the closest parking spot near the boat dock. Not many people would be here to take their boats out today in this frigid weather. As soon as I turned the car off, Pepper was already in my lap and waiting for me to open the door. He bolted out of the car, not waiting for me, as he did every day. Then he darted up the ramp of the boardwalk, where I'd meet him at the front door of the Bean Hive.

The boardwalk was safe, and I was already armed with pepper spray. Patrick had given it to me after I was subjected to an arson a year ago at my cabin. Someone had lit my Christmas tree on fire. But I tried to put those past situations in the back of my mind because I was moving forward and not living in the past.

Briefly, I stopped and looked at the display window of the first shop on the boardwalk. The store was Wild and Whimsy, the local antique shop owned by Beverly and Dan Teagarden. My eyes feasted on the Christmas display in the window. It was an antique table set for the holiday feast with festive wear and adorable mini light-up Christmas trees lined up in a row, along with wreaths tied on the back of each chair.

"I shouldn't've stopped," I said to myself and filled my head with ideas for the Christmas dinner I was hosting for family and friends at the Bean Hive.

The next shop was the Honey-Comb Salon, which reminded me I was in desperate need of a holiday trim. The Buzz In-and-Out Diner was next, and the small light on in the back of the diner told me they were getting ready to open in about an hour, so I hustled on down the boardwalk because I, too, had early customers and the coffee had to be turned on.

"Hey, buddy," I greeted Pepper at the door of the coffee shop. He jumped up, resting his front paws on the door like he was helping me with the key and turning the knob.

I ran my hand along the inside of the wall beside the door and flipped the light on while releasing a long sigh. It was my happy place, and coffee was my love language.

I peeled off my coat and hung it on the coat rack in the back of the shop where the counter was located. Then I picked up and donned my Bean Hive apron. I moved down the counter and flipped all the coffee and tea pots on to let them brew while I walked to the fireplace. Along the way I stopped at each table to make sure the afternoon high-school staff had fully stocked the condiments there. Your basics: sugars, creamer packets, honey, and various other things. I liked to use those little antique cow cream pourers with real cream from the Hill's dairy farm for each table, but I made sure it was fresh every morning.

With a little bit of kindling and some newspaper, I lit the fire on the first try. On my way back to the counter, I checked the self-serve coffee and tea bars to ensure they were ready to go for those customers who didn't want to wait in line and instead used the honor system by putting their payment in the jar. One aspect of my lawyer days had helped me open the shop—I believed in the honesty and innocence of people until proven guilty. No one seemed to cheat the honor system.

The coffee shop was perfect, and I was beyond thrilled with the exposed brick walls, wooden ceiling beams, and shiplap wall. I'd created the last myself out of plywood painted white to make it look like real shiplap.

Instead of investing in a fancy menu or even menu boards that attached to the wall, I'd bought four large chalkboards that hung down from the ceiling over the L-shaped glass countertop.

The first chalkboard menu hung over the pie counter and listed the pies and cookies with their prices. The second menu hung over the tortes and quiches. The third menu that appeared before the L-shaped counter listed the breakfast casseroles and drinks. Above the other counter, the chalkboard listed lunch options, including soups, and catering information.

Pepper sat next to his bowl, waiting eagerly for his morning scoop of kibble. After I filled his bowl, I pushed through the swinging door to the kitchen area of the coffee shop, where I liked to prepare weekly lunch items and bakery goods, even though there was now a bakery a couple of shops down where the tattoo parlor used to be.

With the oven turned on to preheat, I walked over to the freezer, where I pulled out the already prepared usual fare, like the various quiches, donuts, muffins and cookies. Today called for a comfort day since the death of Ryan Moore made me feel a little off.

"I'll make the burnt sugar cake." I smacked my hands together.

The burnt sugar cake was a long-time family recipe that included a lot of sugar, flour, butter, and cream, all the things that screamed comfort in a delicious piece of cake. I got out a few cake pans, since I would be making plenty for the entire week, and sat them down on the preparation station in the middle of the kitchen. I proceeded to the dry ingredient shelf first and then retrieved the wet ingredients from the refrigerator.

By the time I got all those items, the ovens had reached the desired temperature and I was able to get some of the frozen items in the oven to start baking.

"Good morning," I heard Bunny Bowoski call out from the coffee shop.

"I see you, Pepper," Mae Belle Donovan echoed.

Their interactions put a smile on my face. I loved how Mae Belle was such a best friend to Bunny. She was also in her eighties but wasn't employed by me. Still, Mae Belle came to the coffee shop with Bunny in the early hours when Bunny was the one to open, which was today.

Even though I wasn't due to come in until a little bit later, when I couldn't sleep, I usually got up and came on in.

Bunny was probably closer to eighty than not, but she was a regular with nothing to do. She made herself at home and ended up helping people while she was here. She was a great baker and loved to gossip, two things this coffee shop thrived on, so I hired her.

"What's wrong?" Bunny pushed through the swinging door with her heavy coat still on, her brown pocketbook in the crook of her elbow, and a hat parked on top of her grey chin-length hair. Mae Belle followed her.

They were always dressed similarly. Always had on some sort of coat and hat, but not just any hat. Today's choice was one of those little discs with netting around it. Something Bunny would've worn to woo men back in the day... after all, they were older.

"What do you mean, what's wrong?" I asked and sifted all the dry ingredients together.

"All my morning chores are done, and the coffee is already brewed. Plus, you weren't supposed to get here until eight. It's five-thirty." She looked past my shoulder and at the clock on the wall. "I'm opening."

Mae Belle gave me a quick hug before she waddled over to the small coffee pot we kept in the kitchen.

"There was bit of an emergency last night, and I couldn't sleep from thinking about it." Not that I was giving up some big secret. I was sure it'd be all over the news.

"Emergency?" She looked shocked.

"I heard something over the scanner last night about that wreck, but they were very vague." Mae Bell carefully sipped the hot coffee.

As I beat in the eggs, butter, and vanilla, I recapped to them what happened.

"Oh dear." Bunny's brows drew together, and she took her own cup of coffee and sat on one of the stools butted up to the counter next to Mae Belle. "I've been getting my meat from them for years. It's a shame he and Jo Beth haven't had a relationship since he married Yvonne."

"Jo Beth didn't care for none of his wives." Mae Belle's face squished like she smelled a skunk.

"Jo Beth?" I questioned.

"His daughter." Bunny took the bobby pins out of her hair and the hat off her head. "That's right, you didn't live here back then. Jo Beth was so mad when Yvonne came around. Said she was a gold digger." Mae Bell nodded. "But she still came around until Yvonne moved the mother in. From what I hear, that lady is my age and in real bad health."

"Bad health?" I questioned because I didn't think Yvonne's mom looked sickly, just a little slower than Bunny. They might have been the same age, if I recalled correctly.

"That's a shame." Bunny pushed off the counter and stood. "I sure hate to see anyone go to the grave and have disagreements left behind."

"He has a daughter?" I clearly remembered asking Yvonne if there were any children to call. She said no—just her.

"Jo Beth Moore." Bunny waddled back through the swinging door. "Ain't you listening? Come on Mae Belle."

I hurried and got the ingredients into a few of the pans. Then I stuck those in the oven so I could question Bunny and Mae Belle some more.

"I figured you'd be out here." Bunny had already gotten herself, Mae Belle, and me another cup of coffee. I followed them to the couches and sat down to warm up by the fire.

"I asked Yvonne if I could call someone. She said they had no one, and when I asked about kids, she said they didn't have any." I brought the cup of up my lips and took a nice drink.

Everything was better with coffee. Conversation. Friends. Food. And now figuring out the truth out about Yvonne.

"You know…" I hesitated to tell them but figured what the hell. "Patrick and I actually saw them at the Watershed having dinner next to us. They were in a big fight. There were some not-so-nice things said."

I took a drink.

"Do tell." Bunny leaned in closer to me and drank some of her own coffee. Mae Belle nodded encouragement for me to continue.

"He mentioned something about how she knew this when they got married, and she said how she didn't like it, then he said something about over his dead body." I looked up over the rim at Bunny when I took another sip. "I completely forgot she mentioned something about not putting up with his behavior."

"You don't think…" Bunny hesitated this time, like she wanted me to finish her sentence.

"Somehow she made him crash? Or he drove into the lake on purpose?" I asked.

"Nah," we said at the same time and shook our heads right before the bell of the door dinged.

"Sheriff," Bunny looked over her shoulder. "You're not Looooowretta Bebe."

Bunny was referring to one of our most regular and early-bird clients, Loretta Bebe... "Low-retta," as Loretta would say in her big southern drawl.

"Let me grab you a coffee." Bunny got off the couch and headed over to the counter. "We was just talking about the big goings-on last night."

"That's why I'm here." Spencer threw a look at me. "Can I talk to you in private?"

Mae Belle's eyes shifted between Spencer and me.

As if on cue, the timers on the stove went off, signaling the first batch of frozen items was ready to be taken out of the oven, plated, and put into the glass displays for the customers.

"Here's your coffee." Bunny lifted the cup in the air and set it on the counter next to the cash register. "I'm going to get those out so you two can talk."

Spencer was all sorts of serious. I'd never seen him wait until someone left the room before he questioned me on anything.

"This seems very official." I got up from the couch and walked over to the coffee bar, where Spencer was doctoring up his coffee.

"I'm afraid the preliminary autopsy report on Ryan Moore came back." He slowly stirred the full creamer into his coffee.

"Oh, good. I bet Yvonne will be so happy to be able to make plans for the funeral." I tried to relieve the tension a little, but he was definitely tense.

"I'm afraid that won't be happening anytime soon." He slid his glance over to me. "I'm afraid the toxicology report came back with hemlock in his system."

"Hemlock?" My eyes narrowed. "Isn't it a bit cold and snowy for hemlock to grow?" I asked and looked out at the window as the snow, which was predicted, started to fall.

"That's what is so unusual and why I need to investigate a little more." Spencer took a sip of the hot coffee. "I'm afraid this was a homicide."

"Last night after I cleared the scene and got back to the department, I got a disturbing phone call from Jo Beth Moore." Spencer was giving me details that made me pause.

"His daughter?" I asked, trying to clarify what Bunny and Mae Belle had told me.

"Yes. One of the emergency responders is a close friend of hers, and they told her about her dad. I talked to her for a few minutes, and she told me how Yvonne and her dad had been fighting. She asked me to bring Yvonne in for questioning." He let out a long sigh, like he was gearing himself up to tell me something big. "I didn't think two things about it until I got the hemlock report."

"Wow." I blinked a few times. Suddenly my mind felt foggy. "I'm still trying to process the fact he was murdered."

"Who was murdered?" My aunt Maxi Bloom had used her landlord key to let herself in. She flipped the sign. "You're gonna be killed by the regulars if you don't get this place opened."

A few customers had apparently been waiting outside. I'd not realized it was already six a.m.

"Hold on," I told Spencer and hurried over to the swinging door. When I noticed the shoe shadow coming from underneath the door, I knew Bunny and Mae Belle had been listening to every word Spencer and I had said. "You can stop listening and fill the display counters," I told her through the door. "We've got customers."

Spencer took a seat at one of the tables while I ran up to a few people and some of the others took advantage of the self-serve bars, which was exactly what they were meant for.

"What is going on? What are those two hens listening in on?" Aunt Maxi glared at Bunny and Mae Belle. The three of them were the worst and best of friends. I just had to take them with a grain of salt.

"We was just talking about you frequenting the Moose." Mae Bell Donovan had a glint in her eye like she wanted to know what darn business Aunt Maxi had up her sleeve.

"What? Y'all the Moose police?" Aunt Maxi looked Bunny and Mae Bell up and down with an appraising eye. "Or are y'all trying to be my mother?"

"That's enough, ladies." I let out a dramatic sigh and gave Aunt Maxi the stink eye.

Aunt Maxi pulled off her sock cap and pushed the tips in her hair, making it stand to high heaven. Her hair was bright red, in contrast to the blonde color she was sporting a week ago. I'd like to think the cold weather had given her the rosy checks, but it hadn't. She'd put on a little too much makeup for my taste. She took her hobo bag off from across her body and dug deep in it before she pulled out a can of aerosol hairspray. "What's he talking 'bout? What murder?"

"Last night..." I told her about the accident, leaving out the part about the big fight Patrick and I'd seen the Moores have. "Now, Spencer said he was murdered."

"I bet it was that Jo Beth." Aunt Maxi shook the hairspray.

"You can't spray that in there." I'd told her a million times.

"My place. I can do what I want," she grumbled and pushed the button, letting the heavy hairspray keep her now-bright-red head of hair in place.

"If the health department came in here, you'd get me shut down," I warned her.

"I don't see no one." She looked around to prove the point and kept spraying.

I let out a long sigh.

"I told her the same thing," Bunny whispered on her way past us with some quiche hot out of the oven.

"Of course you did," Aunt Maxi said to Bunny in a sarcastic tone.

"I did, Maxine Bloom." Bunny nudged Mae Bell on her way past. "Didn't I?"

"Mae Belle is your best friend. Of course she's gonna take up for whatever it is your saying." Aunt Maxi rolled her eyes.

"*Ahem.*" Spencer cleared his throat and motioned me over.

"Here." I untied my apron and gave it to Aunt Maxi to put it on. "Wash your hands too."

She shrugged and went about waiting on customers, but not without giving them her two cents on what they were ordering. Aunt Maxi was her own woman, and she was proud of it.

"Why are you here to see me?" I asked Spencer the question I wanted to know most since he'd delivered the bombshell.

"Patrick had mentioned how the two of you overheard a fight between the Moores that was in the Watershed and carried over to the parking lot. Then you saw Ryan Moore swerve a few times before he careened off the road and into the lake. I wanted to get your account of it." He took out the small notepad from the inside pocket of his brown sheriff's jacket and set it down on the table in front of him.

"Roxanne!" Aunt Maxi called my name. When I looked up, she waved me over. "Hurry up!"

"Can she wait until you answer my question?" He shook his head, apparently somewhat fed up with the chaos going on in the coffee shop.

"You've come at a bad time. Is there any way I can come to the station?" I asked. "When it's not so busy?"

I was sure by the crowd already gathering at the coffee shop that word of Ryan's murder had gotten around. Every time a crime was committed in Honey Springs, the town folk loved to gather over coffee and gossip about it. And in the few mumblings I overheard, I'd heard Ryan's name mentioned.

"Fine. But I'm very serious, Roxy. I need your exact account of what happened or what you heard." He put his notepad back in his pocket and grabbed his coffee cup before he stood up.

"Promise. Today." I crisscrossed my heart with my finger and headed over to see what Aunt Maxi wanted.

"Hey, do you mind running over to All About the Details and making sure Babette remembers Christmas Day supper?" I wouldn't have time to remind everyone we'd invited, and Aunt Maxi loved making her rounds to all the shops on the boardwalk, so giving her this job to do was perfect.

"Roxy," a woman gushed from underneath a heavy scarf around her head and large sunglasses, taking my attention away from Aunt Maxi. "I'm so thankful for you."

"Oh. That's exactly why I opened the Bean Hive." I smiled at the woman, figuring she was complimenting me on the coffee shop. "I love coffee so much, and I wanted others to feel the same way."

"No." Aunt Maxi smacked my arm. "This is Yvonne Moore under that get-up."

Yvonne took her glasses off her face, and I recognized the eyes but not the dried version of herself.

"I'm so sorry. I didn't recognize you without wet clothes and it being dark, since it was nighttime." My brows made a V shape. "How are you this morning?"

"Well, it's why I'm here. Can we talk?" she asked, putting her glasses back on her face.

"Of course you two can—in the back." Aunt Maxi took the liberty of answering for me. "Bunny, you and Mae Belle stay out of the kitchen." She wagged a finger at them.

"Sure." I nodded. "Let's go back where we can talk." I motioned for Yvonne to follow me. "How can I help you?" I asked once we were away from the prying ears of the elderly gossip queens.

"It appears my husband was poisoned." She pulled the scarf off her head and the glasses off her face, exposing a beautiful complexion and not one wrinkle. Her hair was much blonder than I'd remembered and styled straight, free of bangs and parted down the middle. She definitely didn't look like the woman from last night.

"I heard it was hemlock poisoning." I didn't wait for her to tell me.

"Is that what the sheriff told you?" she asked. "I couldn't help but see he was here when I came in to see you."

"I'm sorry." I glanced over at the timer just as it went off and walked over to get the items out to place them on the cooling racks. I listened to her while I did my chores.

"I'm afraid the sheriff came over early this morning, and he mentioned how the couple who had found us overheard me and Ryan fussing all night."

"Yes. I didn't mention it last night because it didn't seem relevant." Then I looked over at her, and my jaw dropped.

"Yes. I can see by the look on your face that you must know the sheriff thinks I killed Ryan." She tugged off her gloves. "Ridiculous." She placed them on the workstation along with the scarf and sunglasses.

"I'm sorry." It was all I could say. Then I offered her a piece of the burnt sugar cake, hot out of the oven. "There's no need to thank me."

It wasn't very clear why she was here.

"If you'll excuse me, I need to get these out there and help out." I tried to make my own getaway, but she put her hand out to stop me. "The morning rush can be brutal."

"I heard you were a lawyer, and I want to hire you. It appears as though they want me to come in for formal questioning, and I need someone on my side. You were so helpful last night..." Her voice cracked. Tears gathered in her eyes. "I just don't have anyone to turn to. The company lawyers are his family's lawyers, and well..." She hesitated. "They don't care for me too much. Said I was a gold digger just because I'm fifteen years younger than Ryan."

"I... I'd love to." I had no idea why I agreed. The words just came right out of my mouth.

"Thank you!" She gasped and clapped her hands over her mouth, and then she threw them around my neck. "You were a lifesaver last night and now."

CHAPTER FOUR

"A lifesaver?" Leslie Roarke, the owner of Crooked Cat Book Store a few shops down from me, asked after I'd inquired about any hemlock-related books she might be carrying. She looked up at me and pushed her kinky copper hair out of the way. She opened the jar next to the computer, took out a dog treat, and gave it to Pepper.

"Yeah." I flipped through another book on deadly poisons, scanning the pages for anything involving hemlock. I was careful not to spill the coffee cup I'd brought with me. I'd also brought one for Leslie.

"Have you told Spencer you're going to represent her?" Leslie asked and clicked away on the reference computer that stored the shop's book inventory.

"No. I haven't." I took a deep breath. I loved the smell of bound books almost as much as I loved the smell of freshly brewed coffee.

The Crooked Cat Bookstore just so happened to be my very favorite bookstore on the boardwalk. It was one of the shops at which I had the fondest summer memories. Aunt Maxi would drop me off first thing in the morning, and I was so excited to hang out with Alexis Roarke for the day. She did her work while I sat in the beanbag chair in the display window.

Alexis was Leslie's mother. Unfortunately, Alexis had succumbed to an early death, leaving Leslie the bookshop. Not everyone was a "Leslie fan," but she was kind to me and Pepper.

Crooked Cat was still just as I remembered. The beanbags had been replaced by newer ones. The brick fireplace in the middle was still the focal point, surrounded by comfy chairs and big rugs. The dark shelves seemed to go on for miles and miles with beautiful books lined up. The children's section had small furniture and a puppet stage with a big sign that listed the times of the next puppet shows.

In the back of the store was my favorite section of all, the banned books. Aunt Maxi always said that Alexis liked to cause problems when it came to banned books and loved to let everyone know to buy the banned books first. I remember Alexis had a big stamp that read Banned, and she stamped each book on the inside along with a smiley face.

"I think I have some other books in the back," she called out as she walked to the back of the store, where the office and some storage were located.

Pepper and I made our way back through the bookstore. I took my time.

The bell over the bookstore dinged.

"There you are. Bunny said you'd be down here." Louise Carlton walked in with an animal carrier. "I wanted to drop off this gorgeous angora rabbit we got in over the weekend. She's going to make someone's Christmas very happy. She's the only animal that didn't get adopted during the Pawrade."

"Oh no." I sighed deeply and looked at my friend.

Louise was the owner of Pet Palace. After I'd gotten Pepper, I knew I wanted to help in some sort of way, and volunteering on Sunday nights just wasn't enough. It took a lot of paperwork, but somehow, I got my wish. I'd like to say it happened because I was a great lawyer, but honestly, I think Aunt Maxi could sweet-talk the lips off a hog, so the health department allowed me to have animals in the shop portion of the coffee shop. It was a big secret that I let Pepper in the kitchen with me.

Pepper immediately ran up to the front of the bookshop because he loved Louise just as much as I did.

"How much longer are you going to be?" she asked and slid her eyes to the back of the bookstore when Leslie came back out.

The two women looked at each other, giving what I called the Baptist nod. The courteous smile and slight nod were just a polite southern way of acknowledging someone who wasn't quite your favorite person.

These two women didn't see eye to eye. Their grievance was in the past, and I wished they'd left it there, but they hadn't.

"I'll be down there in a few minutes, but Aunt Maxi is there." I took the book Leslie handed me. "If you want to let her do the intake, that'd be great."

The deal Louise and I had was pretty cool. I was able to feature one animal from the Pet Palace each week. It was great because people who might be potential forever-homes for our furry friends could interact with the animals and see how they'd get along. Coffee and animals, perfect in my eyes.

There was some paperwork that had to be completed along with the animals' records and cute photos we liked to put next to the register. We also kept a donation jar for the Pet Palace there, since the Pet Palace did run on donations.

"Fine." Louise's silver bob swung, and the bangled bracelets underneath her coat sleeve could be heard. Louise loved to wear all sorts of jewelry. "Call me when you get a chance."

"I will." I peeked in at the bunny, who was happily munching on some food. "Awww. How gorgeous."

I could see Leslie rocking back and forth as though she were trying to see the bunny.

"Would you like a peek?" I asked her.

"No." She shook her head and went back to busying herself at the computer.

After Louise left, I headed over to register to pay for my stack of books on hemlock.

"You know, a bunny would be amazing for the bookstore." I saw the total come up on the register, and I shrugged and took my money out of my pocket. "Just think how cute the Santa photos would be with a bunny in there too. Or even the Easter Bunny photos."

"Don't you have some reading to do, Roxy Bloom?" She held the bag of books over the counter. I took them. "If you find another book online you'd like to have, let me know."

"I will." I patted my leg. "Let's go, Pepper."

I stopped at the door and zipped up my coat, giving Pepper one last opportunity to get some good patting in from some of the customers in the bookshop. "Don't forget Christmas Day dinner at the coffee shop," I reminded her before Pepper and I headed back down the boardwalk. We went not only to drop off the books but to meet Yvonne Moore at the station.

At least, I'd planned to do that until I walked into the Bean Hive. There, in the very place I'd escaped my previous life, did my previous life stand in front of me with a cup of coffee in his hand.

"Kirk?" I nearly flung the bag of books at him. Just the sheer sight of my ex-husband made my stomach sour, and no amount of coffee would help that.

"You look fantastic." He hurried over to me and took the book bag.

I let him take the bag, and I unzipped my coat, unraveling the scarf from around my neck, really restraining myself from wrapping it around his neck and choking the life out of him.

"Hemlock." He'd opened the bag and read the title of one of the books. "Does this have to do with Ryan Moore? Are you representing his wife?"

I simply pressed my lips together. My past with Kirk seemed like another life.

"I thought I told you a couple of years ago that I didn't want to see you again." I held up my ring finger. "I'm a married woman now."

"To him?" Kirk asked with a tone of disgust.

"Yeah. Him." I pushed past him and grabbed my bag back while Aunt

Maxi glared at him. "I've forgiven you for the crappy marriage we had where you cheated on me with our client."

The images of him giving a lawyer consult, which wasn't the type of consult I thought he was giving the night he phoned to tell me he was going to come home late, were still stuck in my head after I'd decided to take him supper after I got his call. The consulting he was doing was an altogether different type of consulting from what we even offered... if y'all know what I mean.

"But I still haven't forgiven you for what you did to Patrick when he came to visit me in college." I hung the bag of books and my jacket on the coat rack and took the apron from Aunt Maxi.

"I tried to kick him out." Aunt Maxi couldn't stand the sight of him either.

"It all seems to have worked out now." Kirk drew his hands out in front of him. "You've got the coffee shop you've always wanted and your sassy aunt."

"I've had it." Aunt Maxi pushed up her sleeves like she was going to do some sort of boxing.

"Settle down." I put my hand out to her. "We do have to thank him for me being here."

Granted, it was Kirk I had to thank for pushing me over the edge with his affair and running off to Honey Springs, where Aunt Maxi had encouraged me to open the Bean Hive. I still couldn't help but wonder what would've happened if he'd not run into Patrick on our college campus when Patrick had come to see me and professed his undying love... maybe not undying, but it made for a good story. Still, on that day, Patrick had written me off forever after Kirk told him I wanted nothing to do with him and Kirk was my man. Patrick, being the southern gentleman he was, left campus, and I didn't see him until the day I came back to Honey Springs... broken.

"What do you want?" I put my hands on the counter and leaned over.

"I was going to ask you a few questions about Ryan Moore, but in light of the books you've purchased, I now have a lot of questions." He held up the black briefcase I'd given him with his name embossed on the front. The briefcase was so expensive, and I gave it to him when we were graduating from law school. I was drowning in debt but used what little credit was left on my American Express card to buy it for him as a graduation gift.

"Like what?" I wondered how he knew about Ryan Moore. "Are you some ambulance chaser now?"

"Don't be ridiculous, Roxanne." Kirk loved to call me Roxanne when he thought I was being a child. "I'm in town to talk to the witnesses of my clients' sudden death, which we now know was murder."

"Client?" He had my attention.

"Clients," he corrected me. "Ryan and Jo Beth Moore."

"By reason of deduction, I'm thinking Yvonne Moore has called you for legal advice." Kirk might've been a big jerk, but he was a good lawyer.

"Coffee?" I asked, using the "you can get more with honey than vinegar" approach my Aunt Maxi always chirped about.

The right side of his mouth rose in a little grin. He knew all too well how to get my attention when it came to court cases. We might not have made a great couple, but we did make a great partnership in the courtroom.

"You know how I like it." He pointed with the briefcase to a two-top café table near the fireplace. "I'll meet you right over there."

Turning around, I grabbed two white ceramic mugs off the open shelf and stuck them under the industrial carafes. I filled mine to the top and his halfway.

"What is this about?" Aunt Maxi sidled up next to me with the stink eye.

"Jo Beth Moore called him." That was odd, since he didn't even live in our area. "He knows something about Ryan Moore, and he's willing to give it to me."

"There's a catch." Aunt Maxi wagged a finger. "You know it, and I know it."

"Yep." I grabbed both cups by the handles. "I'm going to find out over coffee."

CHAPTER FIVE

It took a lot of deep breathing and slow steps across the coffee shop even to bring myself to look at Kirk as if he had something I wanted to hear. I just wanted to fling the hot coffee all over him, which would bring me a lot of satisfaction.

Able to control myself, I sat the cup in front of him and pushed the condiments toward him. Then I eased down in the chair across from him while I watched him ruin the perfectly good cup of coffee by adding the sugar, creamer, and honey. Didn't he know he could buy a latte with all that in it?

"That was a long sigh." He slowly stirred his coffee and smiled from across the table. "You just really hate me. So you really aren't over me."

"Don't be ridiculous." Honestly, I had no idea he could even hear the internal groans coming from me. "I'm still mad about the lies you told Patrick before you and I were even engaged."

"Listen, I'm not here to rehash old times. Trust me." He picked up the cup and took a sip. "Man, you do make a good roast."

"Stop beating around the bush. What do you want, Kirk?" I asked, not needing the chitchat. I had to get to the station. "I'm busy."

"Busy trying to defend a client that is one hundred percent guilty of killing her husband?" He was using his manipulative ways with me as he carefully crafted his words and slowly took out some file from his briefcase.

"Don't be all professional on me." I glared at him and opened the file he'd pushed across the table. "I know all your little manipulative tricks."

With evident great satisfaction, he sat back in the chair, crossed an ankle on the opposite knee, and picked up his coffee.

"Go on. Read it." He gave that smile I wanted to smack off his face. I'd seen him do it when he knew he had the opposing lawyers in a chokehold they couldn't get out of.

I opened the file and quickly scanned down through it.

"You did Ryan Moore's will?" I asked. "How on earth did he get hooked up with you?"

"More importantly, did you see where all of his money goes to Jo Beth?" he questioned.

"It's not even signed." I shut the file and stuck it back on the table.

"He was signing it today. Convenient for your client to have killed him." He dragged the file back and stuck it in his briefcase. "And we are pursuing murder charges."

"Ridiculous." I scoffed. "She was devastated last night."

So I might've left out that she'd come in to see me this morning.

"Is it?" He leaned up and drummed his fingers on the table. "From what I've read in the police report, you heard them arguing twice, and you saw them go off the road."

"That doesn't make her a killer." I was confident in my statement.

"No, but when you think about it, what did Ryan Moore mean when he said how Yvonne knew this was how it was going to be when she married him?" Kirk grinned. "I have several recorded phone conversations and a videotaped conversation with Ryan Moore on why he wanted to change his will."

"Why did he want to change his will to a daughter who never spoke to him and hadn't in years?" I was willing to play his game. It was still early in the investigation, and I wanted to see his hand.

"Simple. Grandchild. Jo Beth Moore is pregnant, and after she revealed it to her father and Yvonne Moore, he contacted me and told me all about it." Kirk ran his finger around the rim of the cup. "That's when I had him come into the office and tape his wishes. Then I drew up the will and had it ready for our appointment today."

I gulped. Kirk did have a sudden case against Yvonne, and it would take some of my amateur sleuthing skills to help figure out why Ryan would even do such a thing. Part of his estate, maybe, but the whole thing going to a daughter who didn't care for his wife—that was fishy.

The bell over the coffee shop dinged. To buy some time to let what Kirk had said sink in, I looked up to see who it was and caught Patrick's stare. His eyes lowered when he saw I was sitting with Kirk. It didn't take two seconds for Sassy to sniff me out. She came running over and stood next to me.

"Whoa!" Kirk put his hands in the air when the big standard poodle turned around and snarled at him in a way that showed a little teeth.

"No, Sassy." I put my hand on her head. "Be a good girl," I snapped. She sat down.

"Here you go, Patrick. A piece of burnt sugar cake for my favorite nephew." Aunt Maxi showed her love for Patrick in an over-the-top way just to make Kirk uncomfortable. She must've seen Patrick coming in from the outside and had a nice big Red Velvet Crunchie for him. "They are so good today. I think Roxy did an excellent job. She loves you so much."

"What are you doing here?" Patrick took the plate from Aunt Maxi but quickly set it down on a table. He kept his eye on Kirk. "I thought I made it perfectly clear a couple of years ago that you weren't welcome in Honey Springs or the Bean Hive."

"I'm here to help your wife and you about my client's untimely death since you were witnesses." Kirk stood up, and memories of the last time these two stood toe-to-toe flooded back like a nightmare.

"You're nuts if you think I'm going to talk to you." Patrick's shoulders drew back, and his chest popped out.

"Stop it." I jumped up and planted myself between them. "We will talk to you after we are subpoenaed to do so."

"Don't say I didn't try to warn you, Roxy." Kirk didn't bother looking at me. He kept his eye on Patrick.

"Roxanne," I corrected him. "Only my friends call me Roxy."

As Kirk made his way to the entrance, Patrick hollered, "Cane! Roxanne Cane!"

Kirk turned around and gave me one last look before he bolted out of the door into the frigid air. A cold chill swept across the floor and crept along my skin, forming goosebumps. These goosebumps went clear to the bone, giving me pause.

I'd love to say that Patrick was happy with me taking Yvonne Moore on as a client, but he wasn't. After Kirk had left the Bean Hive, Patrick asked me a million questions about why I needed to do that. "Let the law take care of it" was his take.

"I am part of the law," I told him and took the apron off so I could go to the station. "I might be crazy, but I told her I would come down there with her."

"Does Spencer know?" Patrick asked.

"No." I zipped up my coat and looked over at the dogs' bowls to make sure they had water. Sassy and Pepper had gotten in their beds and were asleep right next to the bunny's cage Louise had left.

"He's going to tell you it's a conflict of interest. And look what happened last time you put your nose into a murder." Patrick didn't need to remind me.

"It's fine. I'm looking into it for her and making sure the police do a thorough job." I made it sound so professional and avoided going all in, but now that Kirk was here, I wanted to go up against him, even though I knew I had a tough road ahead of me.

"It's fine that she never mentioned the daughter?" He looked at me with furrowed brows.

"Did you know about Jo Beth?" It suddenly hit me that Patrick probably knew all about the Moore family.

"Of course I did, and she was shocked. I never figured she'd leave out the stepdaughter." Patrick shook his head. "There's something really bad that makes this whole thing stink."

"I'm not disagreeing with that, so I'm just looking into it after I go give my statement." I tried to bring his worried face to ease. "You told Spencer about the fight at the restaurant and how Ryan mentioned 'you knew this before we got married,' didn't you?"

I wanted to be armed because I was certain that was how Kirk had read the reports.

"Yeah. I told them everything. Now the guy was poisoned. Be careful with Yvonne," he warned. "There was a lot of stuff going on about her. Gold digger stuff."

I didn't even ask him what it was because I knew if the public already thought that about her *and* the will was being switched to the future grandbaby, then it certainly didn't look good that Ryan had shown up poisoned. It definitely made Yvonne look guilty, and it was my job to find other suspects.

"I'll be fine." I looked over my shoulder at Bunny. She was making more coffee and cleaning down the counter since the breakfast rush was over. "Will you be okay until lunch?"

"I'll be fine, honey." She winked and shooed me out along with Aunt Maxi and Patrick.

CHAPTER SIX

"You're honestly going to take her on as a client?" Patrick asked me.

Patrick and I weaved in and out of the crowd as we made our way to the parking lot. Sassy and Pepper ran ahead of us.

The boardwalk was filled with holiday shoppers and people taking photos next to the photo booth the Beautification Committee had rented. A photo with the backdrop of Lake Honey Springs was a fun souvenir for tourists to take home along with all the decorations from the Logsdon Landscaping Company.

"I'm going to see what she has to say." There was not a definitive yes or no for me. "In light of her lying to us about children and the fact Ryan changed his will… well… let's just say I will need her to clarify a lot of things before I commit to representing her if it does go to trial."

"Right here at Christmas?" Patrick asked.

"It's not going to take any time away from Christmas," I assured him. "Look!" I pointed at the air. "Snowflakes."

"We still need to decorate our tree." Patrick walked me to my car. "Can we please do it tonight?"

My mind shifted from murder to Christmas. Instantly, I felt much lighter.

"Be sure to remind any of our friends about Christmas Day dinner," I told him.

"I will." He put his arm around me when we stopped at my car. "I know you have that curiosity button on about Ryan and Yvonne, but please don't be late coming home tonight."

Curiosity was my greatest vice.

"Right now I'm going to go to the sheriff's department to give Spencer my account of things and see Yvonne, finish up at the Bean Hive, and then come right home." When I went to give him a kiss, he had a strange look on his face. "What?"

"I don't know. I guess I'm all flustered about Kirk showing up." Patrick played with a couple of my curls. "I saw you two, and it just threw me for a loop."

"Patrick Cane." I held my ring finger in the air. "I'm all yours, whether you like it or not."

I threw my arms around his neck and gave him the biggest kiss, one that must have left him with no doubts about who my man was and always would be... outside of Pepper of course.

I waited until he had the dogs in his truck before I pulled out of the parking lot and headed to downtown Honey Springs.

The boardwalk was only about a three-minute drive to town, seven if it were any other season and I could ride my bike. The cozy town was so charming, and with the revitalization of the boardwalk, Honey Springs had flourished into a great community.

The first building when you drove into the downtown area was the Honey Springs Church, where you could pretty much find every single citizen of Honey Springs on Sunday morning. Next to the church were the firehouse and police station, where I was going. Across the street from that was the Moose Lodge, which stood before the big circle in the middle of town. This circle was known as Central Park.

Along Main Street were the Brandt's Fill 'er Up, Klessinger Realty, the courthouse and its adjoining city hall, Donald's Barber Shop, and the local community college. Other shops around Central Park twinkled with Christmas lights and window displays of all things holiday.

When I pulled up to the front of the sheriff's department, Yvonne Moore was already standing next to the door, waiting for me. This time I wasn't fooled by the big sunglasses.

"I was afraid you changed your mind," Yvonne eagerly greeted me.

"Why would I do that?" I looked at her. "Maybe because my ex-husband is going to represent Jo Beth Moore with the new will your husband had him make up along with video footage of Ryan telling Kirk what he intended. Or the fact that there is a daughter when you clearly told me last night you had no children." I sucked in a deep breath. I could see the information all hit her at once. "Let's get one thing straight." I held up a finger. "I expect any potential client to be one hundred percent truthful with me. There are no excuses. No little lies here and there. I maintain that a lie, no matter how big or small, is a lie."

"I didn't lie to you. I don't have children. You asked if I had any children you could call. Why would I tell you to call Jo Beth when she's not been around and she knew once she was pregnant that Ryan would change his will? So she got pregnant by a disgruntled employee who knew that Ryan wanted to pass the company down and decided to conspire with Jo Beth to make our life a living hell."

Her words fell over me like a weighted blanket.

"I'm sorry," I quickly apologized and realized Kirk showing up out of the blue had a greater impact than I'd thought it had. "I haven't even gotten to hear your side of things. Why don't we walk over to the gazebo in Central Park and talk before we go in there?"

She nodded, tightening the scarf around her neck.

"Let's start from the beginning. Give me a brief history on your relationship with Ryan and the Moore family." The span of time was very broad but would give me a good sense of how they lived their lives.

"It's no secret I was a kitchen utensil company rep that had Honey Springs for my territory. I sold directly to Ryan. Things like butcher knives, meat slicers, more industrial-type equipment butchers use. He made me laugh. He was charming." Yvonne smiled. It was the first time I'd seen her do it, and it was refreshing.

We crossed Main Street and walked over to Central Park. The stroll over there was actually nice, with the snowflakes fluttering around, the lights strung along the fence around the park, and the gazebo decorated with the town Christmas tree.

She continued, "He didn't want children. I didn't want children. I moved in with him. I thought Jo Beth and I would be great friends. From what Ryan had told me, she was amazing. Girly thing. I had no idea she wasn't going to accept me until I met her, and when Ryan left the room after he'd introduced us, she let me know just how much she'd make my life a living you-know-what."

"Why would she do that?" I asked and took the lead to sit on one of the benches in the park.

"I asked Ryan the exact same question. He immediately called her up and asked her. He never told me what she said. The only thing he told me was if Jo ever had children, he'd leave his fortune to them." She sat down, her knees toward me. "I was fine with that. I had no idea he was even worth that much when I was selling to him."

"He married you anyway? Even though his daughter was against it?" I had to question this because I knew Kirk would be all over the relationship between his client and mine.

"Ryan thought she'd come around." She shook her head. "She never did. It's a shame too. He loved her, but as soon as she got pregnant, she showed up at the door."

"Tell me about it." I wanted all the details about Jo Beth and how she sounded so vindictive, which could be a clear motive to have killed her father. "And the father of the baby."

"Gio Porto is his name. He was Ryan's best butcher. Ryan claimed Gio was buying low-quality meat, and Gio said he wasn't. People got sick. Ryan fired him. Ryan came home one night and said that he found Gio and Jo Beth in his office, rummaging through his desk." Yvonne gnawed on her bottom lip and watched the tourists walk by the tree, stopping for selfies. "They had words. Ryan came home with a black eye. I told him to call the police. He was about to, but Jo Beth showed up at the door. That's when Jo told us she and Gio were an item and she was pregnant."

"So she's a few months pregnant?" I asked.

"Apparently. Ryan told me at dinner at the Watershed how he'd gone to see a lawyer outside of Honey Springs. Kirk something." She snapped her fingers as if trying to remember. "He's bound and determined to keep his promise to Jo after all of these years."

"What promise was that?" I asked for clarification.

"He wasn't there for her as a father, and before me he'd really tried hard to make amends with her. He promised her he'd leave the company to her and her children, signing over the company when she was pregnant."

"Go on." Yvonne's story only made me think Gio and Jo Beth had a great motive to have killed Ryan.

I had found a case of revenge *and* murder at once.

"Ryan said he was going to go the next morning, today, and sign off on the will to change the company. That was the argument you overheard us having. It wasn't that I didn't want him to keep his promise, just put something in place to guarantee the child got the company when the child was of age and maybe went to business college. Something that kept the kid accountable. Ryan wouldn't hear of it." She picked at her gloves. "He said he'd be the child's mentor." She closed her eyes and brought her hand to her head. "Now he's dead. I don't understand."

"I know this is hard for you to even consider, but do you think Jo got pregnant by Gio on purpose? Not only because she knew the agreement but also to sock it to him that the baby's father is someone Ryan fired and got beat up by?" I looked over and put a hand on her.

"I..." She gulped. "I guess it's possible. But..." She blinked. Tears rolled down her face. She looked like she just couldn't believe Jo could be this vindictive.

"I'm sorry, but I have to ask." It was a question I'd hated to ask my other defense clients when I was a full-time lawyer. "Did you kill Ryan?"

"No!" she blurted.

"Do you have any access to hemlock?" I knew this was an odd question considering hemlock didn't grow in the winter.

"I don't even know what hemlock looks like, much less know anything about how to poison someone with it."

But where did I start? Who would know about flowers?

All About the Details!

Babette Cliff, the owner of All About the Details, would know everything about flowers, since she was the only event planner in Honey Springs and did every single event. Surely, she'd come across hemlock before.

"I'm going to call Spencer Shepard and tell him that I will represent you on any sort of interrogation." She looked slightly relieved when I said it.

"What if they charge me with murder?" she asked.

"Let's take it day by day." I didn't want to make a full commitment. I wasn't sure Yvonne was what Aunt Maxi would call, and I quote, "playing with a full deck of cards." I'd yet to get a good reading on her and was still somewhat leery about some of the vague answers she'd given me.

"I'm going to tell him that we will be in tomorrow morning to give your statement. You go home and don't talk to anyone. Understand?"

"Yes." She nodded.

"Do not answer the door or the phone. No one." I made myself very clear. "In the meantime, do you recall anything strange the night of the murder? Where he'd gotten hemlock in his food or drink? Or on his skin?"

I'd not been able to figure out this hemlock poisoning part and how it could happen. Nor had I had any time to read the books I'd gotten from Crooked Cat, but I planned on keeping my head in those books until I understood everything I could absorb about the plant.

"Ryan said he was starving and couldn't wait to eat at the Watershed. He didn't even have his before-dinner cocktail," she recalled.

"I can go over to the Watershed and question them. I do know your waitress, Fiona." I was trying to fit all of this in my schedule for today.

The better prepared I was to see Spencer with her in the morning, the better her chances of getting off that suspect list.

"We also had a guy. He was terrible. He even spilled Ryan's water all over him." She laughed.

"Wait." I smacked my hands together. They stung from being cold. "I remember him. I remember that happening. I can question him too. I'd like to get a list of your house staff, and if you have an employee list for the butcher shop, I'd like that too."

I stood up.

"Sure. You can have full access to Ryan's home office." She stood up. "You can have anything I have access to."

"That'd be great." I hugged her, knowing it was probably not a client-appropriate thing to do, but she needed one. "I'll be in touch later today."

"Okay." She hurried across the street. I watched her get into her car and drive off.

"What was that?" Spencer walked out of the station. "I have been sitting in here watching you two have a powwow and expecting you to come in, and she takes off."

"I can't give you a statement from me." I knew he was going to flip.

"Why not?" He asked.

"I'm not stupid. I know you suspect Yvonne did it, but I'm not so sure. That's why I agreed to represent her during her interrogation. We will be here in the morning." I had to get my P's and Q's ready with this hemlock discovery and didn't know enough to have brought her in for questioning today.

"Geez, Roxy." He ran his hands through his hair before he wiped them down his face. "You've got to be kidding me." His hot breath mixed with the cold temperature, letting steam roll out.

"I'll see you in the morning with my client." I wasn't going to divulge anything.

Nor would I wait for Spencer to process what I'd told him, and I certainly knew this wasn't the last time I'd hear from him.

Now I was determined, and All About the Details was my first stop.

CHAPTER SEVEN

The Christmas Carolers were strolling around and singing some festive carols in harmony when I got back to the boardwalk. Even though we were a destination lake town, many families and couples had come to love Honey Springs for the year-around cabins that were available to rent. Today those tourists were out and about, going in and out of the shops on the boardwalk, which were great for those last-minute gifts they needed for Christmas.

The snowflakes were still batting about with a few peeks of sun here and there appearing through the small cracks in the grey winter clouds. It was getting colder, making the snow stick and creating the cozy Christmas feeling I loved.

I'd stopped into the Bean Hive to get a little treat and coffee for Babette.

"Any news?" Aunt Maxi asked after I walked into the kitchen, where she had taken the liberty to make more burnt sugar cake using my recipe.

Bunny was at the front helping customers.

"I'm going to help Yvonne out during her interrogation. She sure does appear to be the number-one suspect, though I might have a couple more to add to my list." I grabbed a to-go box and cut a couple of slices of one of the cakes on the cooling rack.

"I want you to stick it to Kirk." Aunt Maxi stopped the mixer and walked over to the counter, where she pulled out one of the dry-erase boards we sometimes used for daily specials.

I watched her write "victim," "suspects," and "motive" like she'd done before when we stuck our noses in different investigations.

"Who are they?" She was referring to my comment that I had a few more names to add to the list besides Yvonne.

I laughed and shook my head as I closed the to-go box. I loved how we pretended to be mini-sleuths.

"Gio, the disgruntled employee who Ryan had fired and just so happens to be the father of Jo Beth's baby."

Aunt Maxi jerked her head up.

"Good." She wrote everything down and circled "baby."

"We also have Jo Beth."

"His own daughter? I know they didn't get along, but his own daughter?" she asked again with disbelief.

"Oh yeah. If she got pregnant on purpose with Gio's baby, she'd obviously stop at nothing to get back at her father." I held up two fingers. "Revenge and money."

I could see Aunt Maxi's wheels turning and her eyes shifting over all the things she'd written on the wipe-off board.

"Where are you going?" she asked.

"To find out more about hemlock." I grabbed the box and two cups of coffee to go in a carrier.

"I'll keep figuring on this." She tapped the board with her finger.

Now that we had a couple of other people to look into, I needed to know more about hemlock. Babette Cliff was my go-to gal.

"It looks like I'm in time for a little morning snack," I said to Babette when I walked into All About the Details with a couple of slices of burnt sugar cake and two coffee cups.

"You're a lifesaver." She was sitting on one of the white couches in the large open entryway of the event planning store.

When you walked in her store, it was like literally walking into a cozy home. Even though there were gray concrete floors, the store had a big cream shag carpet under a coffee table and folded-up quilts on the edge of the other white couch. There was even a large kitchen-style table with table settings at each chair like you'd have in your home.

Beyond the sitting area and homey feel was a large event area with several tables and a stage in the front. Many events were hosted here. In fact, Babette was going to host a big party called After the New Year for the entire community.

The concept was to have a big party after the holidays and the turnover of the new year during which time, as a community, we could start the year off right. She looked like she was knee-deep into planning it.

"It's good and hot too. I just picked it up on my way over." I set the coffee and treat on the coffee table.

"Thank you." She uncurled her leg from underneath her and reached over to grab the cup. "Planning my own event is more stressful than anything I've ever done."

"I'm sure it's going to be perfect." I couldn't help but notice some of the drawings she'd sketched out. "But I totally understand, which reminds me—you are coming for Christmas Day supper, right?"

I pinched off a piece of the burnt sugar cake and popped it into my mouth.

"Yes. I'm looking forward to it. I can't wait to spend the day with my friends." She sank her teeth into the sweet treat. "Delicious." She picked up the coffee and took a sip. "Oh dear. A little caramel?"

"My Jingle Bell Blend." I always loved coming up with new coffee blends for the holidays. Christmas was so much fun because there were so many flavors to play off and use. "I wanted to pick your brain about something."

"Oh yeah?" She eased back into the couch cushions and held the cup in both hands.

"Hemlock. What do you know about it?" I asked.

"You know the little white flowers along the Lake Honey Springs going past your cabin? Kinda looks like Queen Ann's Lace or maybe baby's breath?" she asked, and I nodded. "That's actually hemlock. It's all over Kentucky, but I know the city really tries to make sure the transportation department mows it down or at least tries to destroy it. But it's hard, so making the public aware of the difference is a life-or-death situation."

"Is it still poisonous if it's dried or dead?" I asked since it was winter and everything on the banks looked to be dead and brown or covered in snow.

"Sure. It's poisonous no matter what form." She narrowed her eyes. "Does this have to do with Ryan Moore? I heard someone saying he was thought to have been poisoned."

"Yes." I gave her a quick rundown on how Patrick and I had found the Moores in the lake. I included a little background on why I was asking about the hemlock, leaving out any details that were within client confidentiality. "Somehow Ryan got something with hemlock in it."

"The plant itself produces over one thousand seeds, and someone can keep those seeds. Most of the farms around here check almost daily for any signs of hemlock because the seeds get mixed into the grass and cause a lot of animal deaths." She took a drink. "It's a pretty horrific death, from what I've heard. People who have been poisoned go into convulsions. They have a lot of saliva."

"I need to check the Moore property for hemlock," I said and noticed the look on Babette's face. "What?"

"I know you're not from here, but from what I remember, Yvonne was not welcome into the family, and I heard he'd changed his will, giving her nothing. I can see her doing it," she said.

"Aunt Maxi?" I asked with a cocked brow.

Babette smiled from behind her coffee cup.

"Thank you for answering my questions about hemlock. I have a stack of books to look through, but I knew you'd give me a good start." I got up from the couch. Sassy and Pepper popped up from the shag rug. "I'll see you on Christmas Day. Let's go," I told the fur babies.

There were a few people on my list to see, and that included Jo Beth, who would wait until after lunch.

Since the Bean Hive was truly a coffee shop and food paired well with coffee, I did offer a light lunch, but those who wanted something bigger could go to the diner on the boardwalk. I only offered simple things like soups, hashes, and casseroles that were easy to make. Whatever I made was the only lunch item the entire week.

I had about fifteen minutes until the lunchtime crowd started to come in for about a two-hour period, and I was happy to see Bunny had already changed the chalkboard to reflect the weekly lunch special, which was potato chowder. Just thinking about it made my mouth water.

"How's it going?" I asked Bunny, who was holding the cute rabbit Louise had dropped off.

"This cutie has gotten a lot of attention. I don't think she's used to it." Bunny pulled a carrot out of the pocket of her apron.

"Maybe someone will take her quickly." I used two fingers to rub down the bunny's head. She jerked her head up, sniffing my fingers.

"Any news on the murder?" Bunny asked. She put the rabbit back in the cage before she followed me through the swinging door to the kitchen. She picked up a book from the counter and handed it to me.

Inside was a Post-it Note from Lesley at the Crooked Cat. The book, which she'd found in the back, was all about the effects of hemlock poisoning and how much was needed to get into the body's system until it killed.

"I think Lesley really likes the rabbit." Bunny smiled. "So tell me what you found out about the murder." She looked over at the whiteboard Aunt Maxi had started.

I glanced over her shoulder at it.

"There's only one person who can really clarify a lot of this," I told her.

"Jo Beth?" She questioned.

"Mmmhmmm," I hummed. "I think I'll just go see Jo Beth myself." The ding over the coffee shop door signaled a customer. "You grab the bread for the soup special, and I'll go see who it is," I told Bunny. She looked comfortable sitting in the chair, and sometimes I worried about her age and if she was working too much.

I rubbed my hands clean on my apron and pushed through the door. Aunt Maxi was helping herself to a piece of quiche.

"It's just you." I walked over, and on my way I grabbed a plate and handed it to her. "Use a plate and enjoy."

"I'm good." She tried to push the plate out of the way, but I insisted. "I wanted to tell you that I heard something about a girlfriend while I was snooping around," she said.

"Girlfriend? What are you talking about?" I asked and poured us a couple of cups of coffee. I had a few minutes before the lunch rush would start. "Let's go watch the snowflakes."

We walked up to the long bar that was the length of the front of the coffee shop. There were stools all lined up so customers could sit there and look out the window at the gorgeous lake or just get some natural light while they read.

"Ryan's girlfriend." Aunt Maxi's words hit me like a lead pipe. "He's been fooling around, and I heard Yvonne had threatened to leave him. Just found out about it a couple nights ago."

"Really?" I asked. "I met with Yvonne a couple hours ago, and she never mentioned a word about it. She made it seem like the entire thing pointed to his daughter getting pregnant by a disgruntled employee—though she did comment to him that she wasn't going to put up with his behavior anymore."

"Yvonne Moore has been pretty proactive in trying to clear her name instead of being a grieving widow." Aunt Maxi was right. "Think about it. She has this public argument with him. They have a car crash because he was poisoned by hemlock."

I needed to find out exactly how long that had to be in your system before you died. It was on the list.

"She showed up here immediately after the sheriff told her Ryan was poisoned, not accusing her of it. She's trying to get a leg up, and maybe she did do it." Aunt Maxi just had to put that in my head.

"That's why I have to find Jo Beth. I think she has a lot of answers to my questions," I said, confirming my next step.

"I know Jo Beth pretty well. When I taught Sunday school, she was in my class." Aunt Maxi finished off the last bit of the quiche and put the fork down on the plate. "Plus, she's cleaning a rental for me today."

She grinned at me. We both looked over our shoulders when we heard Bunny come in from the kitchen. She held the ceramic bowl that fit inside one of the many Crock-Pots I had already lined up behind the counter. My idea was to put the potato chowder in those pots so we didn't have to keep going back into the kitchen whenever someone ordered it.

"I called her a few hours ago, figuring you were going to need to talk to her if you wanted to represent Yvonne but more importantly to stick it to Kirk." Aunt Maxi picked at the edges of her hair, getting it to stand up even higher. She pushed her plate for me to take.

"Your legs broke?" I teased.

"You sassin' me?" She wagged a finger.

"Of course not." I laughed and stood up to take her plate to be washed. "You're going to take me to see her?"

"Nope." She shook her head. "I'll help Bunny out here."

"I don't need your help," Bunny called out. "Whenever you offer to help me, you get me in more trouble than is worth it."

Bunny and Aunt Maxi had never been the best of friends, but at least they weren't at each other's throats like they had been when I moved to Honey Springs.

"I'm still staying." Aunt Maxi winked.

"Don't you dare make my employee mad." As I kissed Aunt Maxi on the head, a few customers came in. "Good afternoon," I greeted them. "Take a seat anywhere. I'll put this plate away and grab a couple of menus."

"Sit by the fire with a bowl of Roxy's potato chowder," Aunt Maxi suggested to the couple. "It'll warm your bones right up."

CHAPTER EIGHT

Jo Beth just so happened to be cleaning a house in the downtown neighborhood. Since the boardwalk was on the way home, I left the dogs at the coffee shop and planned to pick them up on my way home.

"Hello!" I hollered into the house when I opened the door. I heard a vacuum running. "Jo Beth?" I called out louder.

I stood there for a few seconds and realized she couldn't hear me. I took my boots off and stepped into the hallway.

"Jo Beth?" I called toward the noise of the sweeper. When she didn't answer, I walked back into the bedroom, where Jo Beth was bebopping to some music through her headphones while she vacuumed.

"Ah!" She screamed and dropped the handle when she saw me. "Who are you?" She reached down and grabbed the vacuum handle again.

"I'm sorry I scared you. I did call out," I quickly tried to explain as I watched her pick up the vacuum like she was going to use it as a weapon. "I'm Maxine Bloom's niece."

"You got my money?" she asked. Her long black hair was covered with a handkerchief neatly tied around her head. She wore a pair of overalls and Converse tennis shoes.

"Money?" I questioned.

"She owes me for cleaning today." She put the vacuum handle down and her hands in her pockets, making the jean material taut over her pregnant belly.

"Yeah. How much does she owe you?" I could get out some cash from my car if it would break the ice.

"One hundred for today. Don't stiff me. I've got to pay my lawyer. So I'll be done in a few minutes. I vacuum last." She went to flip the vacuum back on.

"I'm not here to pay you, but I've got the money. I'm actually here to talk to you about your dad." Her eyes questioned me. "In full disclosure, I'm looking into things for Yvonne."

"Kirk told me you might come see me." Her eyes narrowed. "Get out."

"Listen, either you can answer my questions now, or I can dig up all sorts of dirt and drag it through the court. I simply want a few questions answered." I had no idea what kind of dirt she had, but I was pretty good at reading people, and she looked like she had a full past she kept swept under the rug. "Is Kirk representing you?"

"He's representing my father." She effectively opened the door for me to ask some questions. "No matter what Yvonne told you, she only married my dad for his money."

"I know you say that, but your father told her your children would inherit the company. What I think they questioned was the father of the baby." She glared at me. "I'm not saying you and Gio don't love each other, but I do think it's possible you got pregnant by him not only for you to get back at your father for marrying Yvonne but for Gio to get back at your father for firing him."

"You have some nerve." I couldn't miss the flare in her temper. "You have no idea how much I helped my father with his company—and for him to discard me when he got married, not to mention Gio. My dad claimed Gio was buying low-quality meat because Yvonne's mother got sick after eating some beef Dad had brought home."

She picked up a few of the cleaning supplies that were on the floor and put them in the bucket.

"If anything, I thought this baby was going to bring me and my father closer after Yvonne had taken him from me." She looked at me. "I love my dad, even though he could never be faithful to my mom or Yvonne."

"Are you saying your father was having an affair?" I asked, since Aunt Maxi had mentioned the idea and now so was Jo Beth.

"Of course he was. That's why he really fired Gio." She shook her head. "Gio caught Dad and his mistress in his office one late night. The meat-truck driver had called and told Gio he was running late. It was Gio's job to check the inventory. He was a manager and had his own key. He said he went to put the invoice in Dad's office, and that's when he found Dad and Abigail."

"Abigail?" I asked.

"Abigail Porter." Jo Beth's brow rose.

I gulped. I still couldn't help but get a gut check when it came to Yvonne and the possibility that she wasn't disclosing the truth.

"Did Yvonne know about the affair?" I asked.

"I don't know. Gio and I didn't tell her. But from that point on, Dad kept close tabs on Gio and made sure to document any little thing Gio did wrong or not the way Dad liked it." She unplugged the vacuum and rolled up the cord.

"Let me help you." I picked up the vacuum when I noticed she was starting to clean up her things.

"Thanks. I'm going to put them in the car." She seemed like a nice girl to me. A little lost and rightfully so, since she'd just lost her dad. "But you know, even though Sheriff Spencer Shepard cleared me and Gio, I still think he thinks I did it."

"You talked to Sheriff Shepard?" I asked.

"Yvonne didn't even call me about my dad. A friend of mine did from the squad." Her voice cracked. "She didn't even have the decency to call me."

That was another gut punch I was trying to get over. Though Yvonne had told me why she didn't tell me about Jo Beth because she wasn't her daughter, she still should've called her.

"My dad and I met for lunch the other day. He gave me the name of the lawyer and his phone number so when the lawyer called, I'd take the phone call. I knew Dad was working it out so my baby and I had a future. Yvonne had no clue what Dad was coming up with. She actually gave him the idea to be my mentor and my baby's. Now I think she's screwed it up by killing him." Jo Beth's eyes filled with tears. "Granted, there were a lot of things I didn't do right when I was growing up and people I wasn't the nicest to, but my dad always helped me see better in people. He might've been upset with Gio and rightfully fired him if Gio had ordered the low-grade meat, but Dad was willing to give him another chance because I love Gio."

I knew it was an awkward time to even bring up the subject, but we were limited in our time together.

"You don't think Gio killed your father?"

"What benefit would that have?" she asked with furrowed brows as a tear rolled down her face. "Dad was going to give Gio another chance, and Gio knew it. Besides, Gio knows that if I ever found out anyone did anything to my father, they'd be cut from my life as well. Gio was very excited about the baby and our future before my father's murder. We were together on the night of my dad's death."

"Your dad was poisoned, so it could've happened over a period of time." Then it hit me. Who on earth did Ryan Moore hang around with the day of his murder?

I had no idea, but I had seen with my own eyes Ryan Moore eating at the Watershed.

Suddenly, I had the urge to grab an afternoon cocktail at the Watershed bar.

CHAPTER NINE

"Uh-oh." Fiona's reaction was pretty priceless when she saw me walk into the bar of the Watershed. Her black hair was down from the normal low ponytail she wore when she was waitressing. "There must be something wrong if you're coming in here in the afternoon."

"What?" I winked and pushed back a strand of my curly hair. "Can't a gal get a drink when she wants one?"

"Coffee?" Fiona laughed.

"I'm afraid you know me all too well." I sat down in front of her and watched as she carefully twirled one of the glasses around the dish towel to dry it.

"I know of a great little coffee shop just down the boardwalk that serves one hundred times better coffee than that old coffee pot back there." She nodded behind her and picked up a beer mug from the dishwasher caddy to dry. "You might've heard about it. The Bean Hive."

"Yeah." I played along. "I went there once. Meh." I shrugged, laughing. "Actually, I wanted to ask you a few questions about the other night when Patrick and I were eating supper."

"The same night the Moores were here?" She put the glass and the towel down and leaned her hip on the bar. "Spencer Shepard was in here earlier asking the same thing. What gives?"

"I'm sure he told you Ryan Moore's death has been ruled a homicide." I waited for her to confirm with her head gesture. "He was poisoned."

"Really?" Her jaw dropped, and her eyes flew open. "No wonder Spencer asked for the receipts when I couldn't remember what they ordered. And he was insistent on making sure I recalled if they'd had cocktails. The Moores never drink. Only water." Her chin slowly turned, and she twisted her head away from me, her eyes narrowed. "What's it to you?" she asked.

"I'm going to be looking into things for Yvonne Moore." I waited for her to respond. Exercising this kind of patience was a trait taught in law school. Actually, it was very important for lawyers to be able to sit, listen, watch, and see how people responded. Now that I'd told Fiona what I had to do with the situation, I hoped she'd start talking.

"I told Shepard they didn't order anything off menu or that had to be made special. No drinks. Just water." She looked over when a customer walked in the bar. "Hey, Jimmy. Your usual?"

The customer, Jimmy, who she obviously knew, gave her a quick yep.

"What about the waitstaff that night?" I asked and watched her grab a small cocktail glass and pour in a four-finger bourbon, no ice.

"Usual." She walked the drink down to Jimmy and came right back.

"No one new?" I asked.

"Nope. I'm the manager for the waitstaff and bussers. I haven't hired anyone new in months." She pulled out a binder from behind the counter and thumbed through it. "Here is the staff a couple of nights ago."

She flipped the binder around. I scanned down the page and noticed the waitstaff's phone numbers were next to their names.

"Can I get a copy of this?" I asked after I noticed the only guy on the page was Pat Frisk. He had to be the busser who'd spilled the water all over Ryan Moore. Bussers were great at listening, and I couldn't help but wonder if Pat had overheard some of the low-whispering fighting the Moores were doing that night.

"Why?" she asked, as she should have.

"I would like to talk to all of them to see if they heard or saw anything. Every little detail is important." It was true. I'd found in past cases how the smallest of clues gave way to the biggest cracks in cases.

"Sure." She took the binder. "I'll be right back."

While she went to make me a copy, I grabbed one of the hemlock books out of my crossbody and flipped to the index in the back. I drew my finger down until I came to the poisoning section, then flipped directly to that chapter.

"What'cha reading?" Fiona asked and slid the copy of the binder next to me.

"Hemlock. Ryan was poisoned from hemlock." My words made her shudder.

"This time of the year?" she asked in a troubled voice. "Hemlock doesn't grow in the winter, especially with snow on the ground."

I turned to look out the window. The snowflakes that had been dancing about in the wind had turned to much larger ones that were sticking to the ground.

"Someone has access to hemlock, and I've got to find out who," I told her and read out loud. "According to this book, hemlock poisoning can take place over days. Or, if in a large dose, it can take six hours."

"I grew up on a farm outside of the lake and hemlock grew all over. My daddy spent half the summer trying to get rid of it before our cows ate it and died." She let out a long sigh. "My brother ate some once, and I'll never forget it."

"What happened?" I asked.

"My parents had rushed him to the hospital and had his stomach pumped out. He was sick for days after that." She frowned as the memory came back to her. "That's the year my mama made my daddy sell the farm. And the beginning of the end of their marriage."

"Gosh. I'm so sorry." I was saddened to see the somber look in her eyes.

"It's all good." She grabbed the bourbon bottle by the neck and a shot glass on her way back down to fill Jimmy's glass.

Fiona must've had a deep hurt that she felt the need to cover up. She filled up Jimmy's glass, the shot glass, and they clinked them in the air before sucking down the brown liquid.

I picked up the piece of paper, stuck it in the hemlock book, and then stuck both in my crossbody. I got off the stool.

"Thanks, Fiona," I called when I passed her and Jimmy.

"No problem. I hope I helped." She offered a smile.

I took my time walking over the metal bridge between the water and land that led to the Watershed. Since it was a floating restaurant, the bridge or a boat was the only way to get to it. I pulled up the edges of my coat around my neck before I grabbed on to the rails. The temperature was below freezing, making the wet snow turn into patches of ice.

Once I got to my car in the parking lot, I decided not to go back to the Bean Hive. Bunny would already be gone and the afternoon help would be there. I'd assess the roads from here to my cabin to make the call if we needed to close down. The staff was my number-one concern, and I certainly didn't want them to drive on icy and dangerous roads.

It was nice to pass a few salt trucks, though I did take it really slow. The roads weren't covered in ice like I'd anticipated them to be. Plus, I'd flipped on the radio station just in time for a weather update. The roads would be icy overnight once the temperatures dropped even more.

After I pulled into my driveway, I grabbed my cell phone and texted one of the afternoon employees to let her know to close early if we only had stragglers coming in. Since there were no planned activities on the boardwalk tonight, I figured the tourists would be nestled in their rented cabins or the Cocoon.

There was nothing better than the smell of a real fire. When I got out of the car, I could not only see the smoke coming from the cabin chimney but smell it. I couldn't help but smile. The freshly fallen snow lay perfect on the roof of the cabin, and the lights from inside glowed.

"I'm home," I sang when I opened the door. Pepper and Sassy ran over to me. Before even taking my coat off, I bent down to let them smother me with kisses.

"Why am I always the last one and get the leftover smooches?" Patrick asked. He was standing in the kitchen with one of my aprons on. He did not care that it was one with lipsticks and lips printed all over it. "Supper is almost ready."

"You're amazing." I unzipped my coat and hung it on the coatrack. I took off my shoes and headed straight over to kiss my husband. "Looks delicious."

"I thought I'd go by Moore's Butchery and get us some chops so I could pan-fry them." They were sizzling in the pan, and the crust Patrick had dragged them in was starting to brown. "Go warm up by the fire and tell me what you found out today."

Patrick's attitude had really changed from a year ago. The first time I'd stuck my nose into one of the sheriff's investigations, Patrick had practically forbidden it. Now he was good at accepting me for me and knew he had to come to love that part of me. It was a part that I'd grown into when we were apart those ten years.

"I'm not even sure how to start." I walked over to the potbelly stove. The window in the door where you put the wood glowed red from the fire inside. On the counter was a bowl of freshly made popcorn that Patrick had already popped for us to make garland.

I sat on the hearth and picked up the needle, thread, and bowl. I carefully strung the needle as I told him about how I'd gotten the list of employees working at the Watershed from Fiona.

Not only had Patrick finished cooking supper, he'd set the café-style table and lit the candle in the middle. Sassy and Pepper had snuggled up on the couch while we ate.

"It was so sad to see her recall how her own brother being poisoned by eating hemlock had led to her parents' divorce." I told him about Fiona's situation. "Very sad."

"Well, I did find out some things." Patrick picked up the wine glass and took a sip, making me wait.

"Some... *things*?" I emphasized the plural.

"Mm-hmm." He took another sip and enjoyed the pain of my waiting. "Gio was there."

"Getting meat?" I asked.

"Nope, cutting it. In fact, he's now head butcher again." Patrick picked up his knife and cut another piece of his pork chop. "Don't you think it's a bit soon?"

"Yeah." My mind was so jumbled with this case. The cause of Ryan's death kept everything from fitting. If it was a clear case of being shot, stabbed, or strangled, it was easier to catch someone without an airtight alibi, but poisoning... it was an altogether different beast.

"What?" Patrick put his utensils down and stared at me. "You've got that look."

"I need to find out who has hemlock stored somewhere. That means I have to go to everyone who had motive enough to kill him and trace their footsteps back for a few days." I knew I also needed to talk to the staff of the Watershed. "I'm going to also go see and talk to all the people who worked at the Watershed."

"How are you going to do that?" Patrick asked.

"I'm going to call them or go see them." Doing that sounded way simpler than it was really going to be. From past cases when I was a full-time lawyer, this type of activity took weeks, and *that* was when I had a paralegal.

I didn't have weeks. Nor did I have a paralegal to help. Thank God, Aunt Maxi was into the case. She'd surely hunt some of these people down. Especially Pat. He was someone I really wanted to talk to since he'd been the Moores' busser.

"Not tonight." Patrick got up and walked over to the box of decorations he'd put next to the tree. "Tonight you're all ours."

"There's no other place I'd rather be." I grabbed my wine glass and walked up to the nice fir we'd picked out, admiring it. It had the perfect stiff needles for the ornaments we'd collected from over the past year in celebration of the life we'd begun.

"I did get something for us today." He pulled out one of those clay ornaments with a man and woman along with two dogs. The ornament was personalized with our names.

"I'm so lucky." I took the ornament and ran a finger over it. "I love it, Patrick Cane."

CHAPTER TEN

There was nothing better than a full belly and the love of your life next to you to help you get a great night's sleep. Or maybe it was that I hadn't slept a wink the night before, but I'll say the warmth of the bed with Patrick, Sassy, and Pepper making it all cozy got me the shut-eye needed to ensure I was wide awake and raring to go when the alarm went off.

"Good morning." I looked up and saw Patrick standing over me with a cup of coffee. "I didn't even hear you get out of bed."

"You were out." He smiled and gave me the coffee once I pushed myself up in the bed.

Sassy jumped off. Pepper stayed tucked in the covers next to me.

"I got a service call from Camey." He had done all the remodeling for Cocoon Hotel, and Camey was great about calling Patrick if something needed to be repaired. "One of their ovens isn't working in the kitchen."

He sat on the edge of the bed and put on his work boots.

"Tell her I'll be down to bring her coffee this morning." I pulled the covers off. Pepper stuck his head out from underneath. "I'm sure Bunny has it all ready. Ask Camey if she needs me to bring anything for her guests to eat."

Not that I had a lot, but I certainly had enough in the Bean Hive freezer to take down to her guests while Patrick fixed the oven.

"I will." He got up, turned, and kissed me goodbye. "You keep your nose out of anything that'll get you in trouble."

I gave him a smile and wink. We both knew I wasn't going to commit to anything that I couldn't guarantee.

"Love you!" I hollered out to him. I pulled the covers back over me when my legs got a chill. "Just a few more minutes," I told Pepper.

He immediately put his head under the cover, apparently thinking it was a great idea.

The coffee warmed me and got my brain in somewhat of a working order. Items on the to-do list I needed to accomplish today started to drift in one at a time.

"We need to go to the Bean Hive and get Camey her coffee for the hospitality room." I was talking to Pepper like he was truly listening, but the light snoring from underneath the covers told me he was fast asleep. Sassy had gone to work with Patrick. "We also need to meet Yvonne at the sheriff's department, which means I need to dress a little better than my regular Bean Hive clothing just in case Kirk shows up."

It wasn't unusual for Kirk to request to be present during a police interview of a potential suspect in a case he'd taken on. In this instance, I was sure he would enjoy having to deal with me.

"He has no idea what he's in for." I drank the last sip of coffee in my mug and put it down on the table. "Let's get moving, Pepper." I threw back the covers and got out of bed, ready to face what the day was going to bring.

It didn't take long for me to take a shower and put on a pair of black slacks with black boots, a white button-down shirt, and a black blazer to match. The long-sleeved Bean Hive shirt would go fine with the pants once I was back to work at the coffee shop.

Patrick had filled Pepper's bowl with kibble before he left, so Pepper ate and waited patiently by the door.

With my overcoat zipped up, I bent down and put Pepper's sweater on him. He loved his sweater. He danced around, his little grey stump tail wiggling as fast as it could go. I gave him a good scratch under his chin and used my fingers to comb down his beard.

"Are you ready?" I asked in an excited voice. I opened the door, grabbed my crossbody, and with my keys in hand, went out the door.

Pepper ran around and did his business while I opened the trunk and got out a blanket for him to sit on since the snowfall was still on the ground. I was happy to see the roads weren't covered, which meant the road crew had done a great job. I grabbed the old briefcase I kept in the trunk I'd used in my lawyer days. Truthfully, there was nothing in it, but I was going to look the part.

Honestly, I'd totally given up on being a lawyer when I moved to Honey Springs, but once people started to find out I was once a lawyer, they did ask me for various services. Unfortunately, this wasn't the first murder I'd come across, though I wished it would be the last.

"You ready?" I asked Pepper again when he got back to the car. I opened the door and fixed his blanket before he jumped in. I used the edges of the blanket to clean off the snow from his fur. If I didn't, it'd clump and hang on the fur.

I slowed the car down when we went around the curve where the Moores had wrecked. The tire marks in the grass were covered with snow, but I knew they were under there.

"We have to figure out where the hemlock came from," I said out loud. Pepper had planted his front paws on the door handle and was looking out the window. "And I need to talk to Abigail Porter."

I didn't want to ask Yvonne about Abigail, her supposed best friend who Jo Beth claimed her father was having an affair with, but if it would take her off the suspect list and put Abigail on as a replacement, I had to do what Patrick asked me not to do… be nosy.

"Something smells good in here." The smell of cinnamon, nutmeg, and sugar filled the air and swept over me when Pepper and I walked in the Bean Hive.

"Good morning!" Bunny called from behind the counter. "You can flip the sign."

I did exactly what she told me to do. We had a few minutes before opening time, and I was glad to see she'd already gotten the display cases filled and the coffee pots all brewed.

"How did you sleep?" she asked and handed me a cup of the Jingle Bell Blend.

"Like a log." I took a sip before I even took off my coat. "It's so cold out. This is so good. Thank you."

"You're welcome, dear." Bunny was buttering me up for something.

"What?" I asked.

"Well…" she hesitated and wrung her hands, looking worried. "I've lost the bunny rabbit."

"What?" I jumped up and put the mug on the counter, then headed straight over to the cage to see for myself.

The rabbit was not in there. I moved the cage. I moved the free-standing coffee station. Nothing. Frantically, I ran around the shop moving things, looking for rabbit poop and anything that looked like it might be chewed on, but nothing.

"I'm sorry. I have no idea what happened." She stood there with the most pitiful look on her face.

"Let's trace your steps." The situation was like a mystery, and I always found in cases that retracing steps was a great way to find… "Bunny! You're brilliant! I have to retrace Ryan Moore's steps for the day."

I ran back to the kitchen and brought out the wipe-off board with the suspects Aunt Maxi and I had listed.

"You're not mad?" Bunny asked with some caution in her voice.

"We need to find the rabbit. Where could've it gone?" It wasn't like we were open, and it also wasn't like the rabbit could open the cage door and walk out. "Tell me exactly what you did this morning."

"My alarm went off, and my arthritis was aching from the cold." She rubbed her elbow.

"No. I'm sorry your arthritis is acting up, but start from when you opened that door." I pointed at the front door of the Bean Hive.

"I opened the door with my key and stuck it right back in my pocketbook." She seemed to be into this sort of questioning. Her voice picked up with excitement as she recalled the facts of how she'd locked the door, hung up her coat, put up her pocketbook, put on the apron, and headed directly to the coffee pots to flip them on. "Then I went back to the kitchen and turned on the ovens."

She had the same routine each of us did when we opened. In fact, I had a checklist posted not only next to the register but on the refrigerator in the kitchen.

She'd done everything on the list, including getting the food ready for the display cases.

"I even put a few logs on the fire." Though she tried to recall what happened to the rabbit, she did have a little pride in that fire. "That's when Lesley Roarke knocked."

"Lesley?" I asked and felt a sense of relief. "You didn't say she came by."

"It's not unusual for the owners of shops to come and grab a cup on their way to their own stores." She was right. Many of the shop owners knew we were there getting ready for our early-morning customers well before their doors even opened.

"I know, but I was just at Crooked Cat yesterday when Louise came down there looking for me to drop the bunny off. I told Lesley a rabbit would be great for the bookstore and especially the children's story time." I smiled. "If I recall correctly, I do believe story time is today." I walked behind the counter and started to look around. "Are you sure she didn't say anything or leave a note?" I asked.

"Not that I remember." Bunny's worried look came back.

A few customers came into the coffee shop. A gust of cold air swept along the floor and circled around me, sending goosebumps all over my body. I smiled at the customers while they looked down the display counter.

"I'll call her." I dug deep into my crossbody and grabbed my phone, only to find a text from Lesley. "Here. She left a text." I read out loud, "Roxy, I decided to give the rabbit a try at story time. Your idea really sounds good. I went to get a coffee from Bunny this morning and told her I was going to borrow the rabbit for the day. Bunny said okay, but she seemed to be occupied with something else, so I'm not sure if she heard me. TTYL."

"TTYL?" Bunny jerked back.

"Talk to you later." Was that really all Bunny had heard from the text? "She said you seemed to be occupied with something else. Are you okay?"

"I'm fine." Bunny shuffled around me. "I'm glad the rabbit is okay."

"Yeah. Me too." Now that Lesley brought it to my attention and I'd asked Bunny, I could clearly see she was hiding or very nervous about something.

That was yet another mystery to solve, but I didn't have time to explore it.

"I'm going to take the carafes down to Cocoon Hotel." I took two of the industrial carafes from the coffee pot and replaced them to fill up. "You okay for a few minutes?"

"Of course I am. I reckon you're gonna be on me now that Lesley said my mind was occupied." Bunny didn't like to have tabs kept on her. She was very proud of her independence. "I won't have none of that. You hear me, Roxanne Bloom?" She shook her crooked finger at me.

"It's nothing I don't ask every time I leave." That was the truth. I always made sure I asked whoever was working with me if they'd be okay when I had to run errands. Only this time, Bunny's reaction did make me think she was hiding something. But what?

CHAPTER ELEVEN

"Good morning." I was caught off guard when Aunt Maxi and I ran into each other as I was leaving the coffee shop. "Want to walk down to Cocoon with me so I can drop off the coffee?"

"I was gonna warm up by the fire." She hemmed and hawed and looked into the window of the Bean Hive. Pepper did look very snug in the dog bed next to the fireplace. "I guess I can." She tugged the stocking hat she had pulled on her head down a little more, covering her ears. She also wore a bright red velvet coat and matching red gloves.

"You'll be fine. Besides, you've got so much red on, you look like you're on fire." I laughed and handed her one of the carafes.

"I can't help it if I'm full of style and glamour." She definitely always dressed eccentrically but in a fashionable way, something I could never pull off.

"What are you doing today?" I asked on our way down the boardwalk to Cocoon. I was glad the snow had melted off the boardwalk. The effect made for a really nice, crisp walk as the dawn started to pop up over the trees. The Christmas lights wrapped around the carriage poles gave off a warm glow. The sights filled my soul with joy, though if I took a second to think about Yvonne, the joy was somewhat dampened.

"What did you hear?" She jerked.

"Are you hiding something?" I questioned her, since her reaction was not like her.

"You rarely ask me that this early." Aunt Maxi shrugged and returned to her normal self.

"I've got to meet Yvonne Moore at the sheriff's department, but I need someone to look into something for me at the Watershed." I'd actually left the copy of who was working at the Watershed that Fiona had given me. "I also need to retrace Ryan Moore's steps for the entire day."

"What's at the Watershed?" Aunt Maxi did seem interested now that she knew it was part of the investigation.

"It can take six to nine hours for hemlock poisoning to go into effect, and if I can trace back Ryan's steps and who he interacted with from that day, I might get a clue to more suspects." It wasn't like I doubted we had a good list now, but Jo Beth, Gio and Yvonne seemed so obvious, and each one had their own reasons.

Though I'd not talked to Gio, Jo Beth was right. Why would he bother getting blood on his hands when he was going to flourish by just being the dad to Ryan's grandchild?

"The last place he was alive was the Watershed. Fiona was his waitress, but there was a Pat working there that night too. He was the busboy. He spilled water all over Ryan, and I just wanted to know if Pat overheard Ryan and Yvonne saying anything. Or really any leads." I knew the event was memorable, so maybe Pat did hear something. Anything.

"According to the schedule, Pat is working the lunch shift today. If you had time, I thought you might be able to stop in before you come to lunch." Aunt Maxi never missed a lunch with me at the Bean Hive.

"I can do that." She gave a hard nod. "But I won't be eating lunch with you today."

"You won't?" I was looking forward to enjoying the scenery of the walkway between the boardwalk and the Cocoon Hotel, but Aunt Maxi shocked me by telling me she wasn't coming for lunch. That ruined it.

"Nope. I've got me a date. Why do you think I've got a little hitch in my giddy-up?" She was awfully giddy for this early in the morning.

"I… I…" I stammered.

"Close your mouth. You'll catch cold." Aunt Maxi picked up her step and hurried in front of me.

I'd not realized how hard I'd gripped the carafe's handle until I made it inside of the Cocoon Hotel and put the coffee down in the hospitality room.

"Are you all right?" Camey Montgomery asked. She wore a festive green sweater with a little white faux fur around the cuffs of the sleeves. The green made her scarlet hair pop. Her thick bangs hung perfectly across her brows.

"Yeah." I worked my hand open and closed. "Aunt Maxi just shocked me by telling me she has a lunch date."

"Really?" Camey had picked up a copy of one of the southern Christmas magazines she had stacked on the table beside a chair near the hospitality room's fireplace and fanned herself.

We both looked at Aunt Maxi. She was helping a guest figure out the coffee carafe to get a cup.

"I'm burning up," Camey panted.

"You havin' your own personal summer over there?" Aunt Maxi asked with a laugh.

"Yes. I think I'm going through the change." Camey shook her head. "You'd think at my age it'd already happened."

"I'm sorry. Maybe it's the stress of the ovens." The suggestion was supposed to make her feel better.

"Patrick is a lifesaver. He has three of his electricians here, and he's back there elbow deep too." Camey turned when Newton Oakley, her handyman for the hotel, walked in and waved her over. "Excuse me. I've got a final meeting this early morning with the Logsdon Landscaping to pay for the decoration near the lake. Have you seen them?" she asked me from over her shoulder on the way out of the room. "Go look!"

Camey disappeared, but someone bigger than life walked right through that door.

"I thought I heard you in here, yapping." Loretta Bebe was dressed to the nines. She had on a houndstooth wool skirt suit. Her black purse dangled over her elbow. She wore pearls the size of baseballs in her ears and around her neck. Her short black hair stood out against her tan skin, something she said was because of her Native American heritage, but we all knew it was from the tanning bed over at Lisa Stalh's house and that tanning bed she kept in her garage.

"Hello, Low-retta," Aunt Maxi's said in her southern "bless your heart" voice. "What are you doing up at this time of the day?" Aunt Maxi leaned over and whispered to me, "She had to get up two hours ago to get into that get-up."

"Oh, Maxine, what's this I hear about you and Floyd? I mean, come on? The thought of Bunny Bowoski's leftovers. Shock-ing." Loretta was poking the bear... Aunt Maxi.

I really wanted to say something, but the shock of Aunt Maxi and Floyd was something I couldn't process. In fact, it left me dumbfounded.

"Don't be jealous." Aunt Maxi winked and watched as Loretta traipsed past us and helped herself to a cup of coffee and pastry. "Besides, that high horse you seem to be on this morning makes your ass look big."

"Aunt Maxi," I gasped and grabbed her by the elbow. "It was so good seeing you, Loretta." I jerked Aunt Maxi. "Let's go."

"What?" Aunt Maxi jerked her arm from me. "I can say as I please and do what I want."

As much as she tried to get away from me, I clung on to her and gripped her tighter.

"What is wrong with you?" I asked once we made it outside on the hotel's porch. "No wonder Bunny is in a weird mood. You stole Floyd from her."

"I didn't *steeeal* anyone." Aunt Maxi drew out her word trying to convince me.

"If I recall correctly, the first time I ever saw you and Bunny interact, she stated you'd been down at the Moose trying to steal Floyd."

Aunt Maxi tried to interrupt me. "And," I said too loudly for her to even think she could say something until I was finished, "You told her not to flatter herself because you wanted a man who could walk without stopping every two feet so he could get his footing up under him so he didn't fall."

"Did I?" She puckered her lips like she didn't remember. Aunt Maxi wasn't fooling me any. She had the mind of an elephant, which supposedly remembered everything… or maybe that was just another one of our southern sayings.

"Yes, you did, and you need to let Floyd go this instant," I demanded.

"I will do no such thing. You need to go back to the coffee shop and simmer down." She was trying to scold me into thinking what she and Floyd had done to poor Bunny was all right. "Now let me tell you something. I sure hope you don't find yourself in my situation." I was sure she was referring to my uncle's passing, leaving her a widow. "But when pickins are slim, you take what you can."

"I'm sure there's more men at the Moose than Floyd." I wasn't going to let her bully me into thinking she was right about him.

"Fine. I won't go back into the Bean Hive." She stomped off once we reached the ramp to the boardwalk. "I'll let you know about Pat."

I shook my head. No matter how she and I clashed about Floyd and her morality, she was too dang nosy to stay away from the little bit of investigation I needed her to do.

CHAPTER TWELVE

Bunny and I got through the morning crowd without talking about what was bothering her, and now that I knew what it was, I decided to let her tell me when she was ready.

The breakfast rush had ended just in time for me to head down to the department to meet Yvonne Moore.

The grey clouds hung low over our small town. They were thick snow clouds, and I was hoping, unlike most of the other residents in Honey Spring, it would be snowy for Christmas. I couldn't see all of Central Park from the parking lot of the department, but the twinkling lights were on, and the Christmas tree stand had people mingling in and out of the firs.

Steam puffed out of one of the vendor tents, which I knew had to be from the freshly popped kettle corn I was smelling. Though I was going into the department to try to defend someone in a murder case, my heart still had the joy of the season.

I was very thankful for Honey Springs and how it'd embraced me. Unfortunately, that joy quickly faded when I jerked around to see who was knocking on my car window.

Kirk.

With a huge smile on his face, he waved. In fear my eyes would get stuck, I refrained from the big eye roll I felt like I was on the verge of giving him.

I opened the door and grabbed the empty briefcase. "Kirk," I said stiffly. "I thought I'd see you here."

"Yes. You do know me." He laughed. "I take no pleasure in taking down your client."

"We will see." I turned and watched Yvonne pull into the parking lot.

When she got out of the car, she smoothed out her black pressed suit coat and the hint of a cream shirt underneath, as if her drive over had sullied them. She gave a quick shake of her hair, but not a strand shifted. She dropped her hands to her side, and with her head lifted, she drew back her shoulders and focused on the door of the station.

"Oh man." Kirk smiled so big. "This is going to be good. See you in there, Roxanne Cane."

I threw him a tight smile before I turned to greet Yvonne.

"So, let me do all the talking. Understand?" I wanted confirmation. She nodded.

I led the way into the department, where Spencer Shepard, Kirk, and Jo Beth were already standing.

It was as if the time had stopped between the two women. Both of them were hurting, and I couldn't help but feel as though the one wanted to reach out to the other and vice versa. But it was Jo Beth who took the deep breath and whispered something into Kirk's ear, at which point he led Yvonne off in a different direction.

"Mrs. Moore. Roxy." Spencer walked over, placing the file up under his arm. "If you two don't mind following me into a room, we'll get started."

"Will Kirk be joining us?" I asked.

"If you'd like, but it's not necessary. I can give him a report of the statement." Spencer had always been fair to me.

"I don't oppose it if Yvonne doesn't." I looked at her.

"I'm fine with it. I have nothing to hide." Yvonne shrugged with the utmost confidence that I loved.

"Bring him in." I stopped at the door of the room and told Spencer, "You sit right here."

I'd assessed the room because I knew exactly where Kirk had always preferred to be when he was involved in client statements. If we occupied his space, he'd be unable to think clearly. It was one of his weirdo techniques he claimed was a key to his success.

Yvonne took her seat, and I plopped the briefcase up on the table.

Spencer and Kirk came in directly. Kirk looked frantically about the room. He grabbed a chair with his hand and began to shift it right then left. He appeared to be in a pickle. He fussed with the chair a few more seconds before giving in and sitting down.

My soul felt a bit of a satisfaction as I watched him squirm.

Spencer sat down in the chair right across the table from Yvonne and pushed the button on the microphone before he pushed it into the middle of the table.

He rambled off the date, time, and case number before he started to ask the usual questions—"state your name, birthdate, address, occupation. How did you know the victim?"

"I understand you and your husband were fighting on the night of the wreck. I also understand you'd told him you were filing for divorce. Is that correct?" Spencer asked.

Kirk shifted in his seat.

"Yes. I did say that." She looked at me, and I gestured okay.

"Why did you say that?" Spencer asked.

"He was having an affair." She lifted her chin. Though she was trying not to cry, I could see the puddles forming in her eyes.

"Do you have any access to hemlock?" Spencer asked Yvonne.

"No," she stated matter-of-factly. "I don't even know what it looks like."

"In these photos we found on your house computer"—Spencer opened the file and took out some photos. He slid them across the table for Yvonne to look at. "The small white flowers are hemlock. And according to Daryl, your housekeeper, she said you pick those all the time around your property."

"I had no idea they were hemlock." She looked at the photos and then eased back into the chair.

"Just because my client picks flowers off her own property doesn't mean she's a botanist. She only likes to make her home pretty. And you know it's hemlock?" I asked Spencer.

"We had some of the dead weeds tested around the property, and according to Logsdon Landscaping, who does all of the Moores' landscaping, they have hemlock on the property." Spencer's words put a huge smile on Kirk's face that I wanted to smack right off.

"That might be the case, but Yvonne has no access to any sort of hemlock that's alive." I shook my head. "If you haven't noticed, it's winter."

"That's where you're wrong." Spencer opened the file again and took out more photos. "Here is a photo of some hemlock in a small greenhouse we seized during the search of the property."

This piece of evidence was hard to swallow. Not only did they have my client fighting with the victim, who'd been caught cheating on her, but they also had the live murder weapon.

"My client Jo Beth Moore would like to bring murder charges against Yvonne Moore for the murder of Ryan Moore." Kirk jumped up and smacked the table.

"That's ridiculous. I didn't kill him!" Yvonne screamed out.

"Yvonne." I tried to calm her, but it didn't help.

Spencer put his hand out to her and Kirk.

"Mrs. Moore, I understand how terrible it is to find out your husband had cheated on you. Trust me, if you just tell us the truth that you did kill Ryan Moore from the hemlock of your greenhouse, we can lessen the charges." Spencer was trying to wrangle a confession from her.

"No way." I shook my head. "My client..."

"I did it. I killed Ryan." Yvonne Moore buried her head in her hands.

A feeling of dread crawled through me.

CHAPTER THIRTEEN

"That was easier than I thought." Kirk took pride in watching Spencer haul Yvonne off to the booking part of the station. "I'm sorry, Roxy. Really. You always tried to see the good in people."

"Yeah. That's why I stuck around married to you too long." I gripped the handle of the briefcase and headed out of the interview room.

The tension began to rise in me from just the sheer knowledge that Kirk was walking behind me. The only bright side to this situation was that Kirk would be getting out of Honey Springs.

"Excuse me. I need to tell my client the good news." He hurried around me, brushing up against me, practically making me sick to my stomach.

I couldn't get out of there fast enough. Once in my car, I grabbed my phone to follow up on what Yvonne had asked me to do when they were handcuffing her.

She wanted me to call her mom and let her know that Yvonne had confessed to murdering Ryan and that the raid had found her hemlock in her greenhouse. "Promise me you'll call her," she'd said.

"Forget it." I threw the phone down in the passenger seat and pulled the back of the bag of Gingerbread Softies.

I took a bite and looked at it. It was the treat I had planned on sharing with Yvonne after we answered Spencer's questions in celebration of the interrogation being over, but the bad taste of seeing Kirk and Jo Beth walking out of the station left a sour feeling in my stomach.

"Forget it." I put the cookie down and threw the car in gear.

There was no better time to eat a cookie than while telling Yvonne's mom what'd happened in person. Besides, if she was as fragile as I'd heard, I wanted to make sure Daryl was with her and she didn't pass out at the news, so doing it in person was a much better idea.

The snow was falling in big flakes, which made me take the roads a lot slower than normal, but it also gave me some time to think.

For someone to be so adamant about not killing her husband, she sure did an about-face, which made me wonder what she was hiding. Really hiding. I had no time to question her, since they were going to take her straight to booking. That would take a few hours. I'd be sure to call and set up a time with the station secretary for talking privately with Yvonne and getting the real scoop.

The Logsdon Landscaping Company must've been finished with the outside decorating because there were lights strung along the fence, along the gate, and around all the oak trees that lined the Moores' driveway.

I rolled down the window and pushed the button on the gate speaker box.

"How can I help you?" Daryl asked.

"It's Roxanne Bloom. I'm here to talk to Yvonne's mom about Yvonne." Immediately the gate buzzed open.

Slowly I drove up the driveway and noticed in the rearview mirror that my tires were leaving tracks. The water fountain was turned off. A big blow-up snow globe feature was in the middle, which wasn't there the other day. Then I thought about Yvonne leaving here this morning. Did she look at the decorations and think of how Ryan loved Christmas? Did she even know she wouldn't be coming back today? Had she planned on confessing this entire time?

Daryl had the door open when I got out. She waved me inside in a hurried fashion.

"Where's Mrs. Moore?" Daryl looked out the door when I stepped into the foyer.

Wow. A huge tree spanned from the floor to the ceiling of the mansion foyer. Clearly it wasn't there when Patrick and I had brought Yvonne home the night of the wreck... or murder.

"Yvonne, honey," I heard Yvonne's mom say before she entered. "I packed up all your warm fuzzy blankets. I need to know—what do you want me to do with all these heels?"

A pair of red snakeskin stilettoes dangled from her fingers, and a towel hung over her shoulder.

"I'm sorry." She looked between Daryl and me. "Did Yvonne go upstairs?"

"Can I talk to you?" I asked.

"Sure. I don't think we were introduced properly the other night. I'm Belinda." She turned to go back to where she'd come from. "We can talk in here while we pack. Daryl, please tell Yvonne the first round of Goodwill will be here soon."

Daryl knew something was up because she followed us into the room where Yvonne had lain down on a couch, but there was no couch now. In fact, there were piles upon piles of boxes.

"I'm sure Yvonne told you that I'm Roxy Bloom. I'm a part time"—I started to say "very part-time but didn't—"attorney. And when she was asked to come to the station to give her statement, she asked me to come along." My head tilted to the right and left. "Just to make sure she was represented."

It was so strange of her to suddenly confess. Why would she bother disguising herself to come to the Bean Hive the next morning and ask me to help her? Something wasn't right, and if Yvonne thought I was going to accept this type of sudden change in plea, she didn't know this lawyer very well. Now I was confident something was wrong.

"Yes." Belinda nodded eagerly. "Excuse the mess. We are moving to a much smaller place. Yvonne can't live without her blankets because, you know, she hates to be cold." I didn't know, but I let Belinda tell me about her daughter, knowing in a few minutes she'd be devastated at the news about Yvonne confessing to Ryan's murder.

Belinda put the shoes down and walked over to the built-in glass shelves that I didn't remember from the other night either. She took down a trophy and pulled the towel off her shoulder to dust off the trophy. She looked at it and smiled. "And she loved her trophies. Those were the days."

She held the trophy in my direction. I walked over and looked at it.

"Championship State in breaststroke," I read off the gold-plated plaque glued on the front.

"Yvonne held the state record for years before anyone beat her." Her mom put the trophy down in the box.

I just so happened to look in and saw many more trophies that must've been displayed on the shelves. Yvonne knew how to swim. My mind curled back to how Patrick pulled her from the water. Wouldn't her keen sense of swimming kick in to help get her own self out of the truck? Did she know Patrick and I were behind them? Did she see us in the rearview mirror, and when Ryan drove off the road, did she figure we'd jump in, and if not, she would save herself, making sure Ryan was underwater for a good period of time and would drown for good measure?

All the reasons why I believed Yvonne Moore didn't kill her husband just flew out of my mind and made me start to think she did kill him.

"Ryan loved looking at her trophies, even though she'd gotten them way before they knew each other." She let out a long sigh and picked up another trophy. "Where is that daughter of mine?" She tilted her head around me. "You know, she's not slept a wink since Ryan. She loved him so much."

"I'm not sure if you knew Yvonne had me meet her at the station to talk to Sheriff Shepard, but she did confess to killing Ryan."

Belinda dropped the trophy, shattering the angel statue right off the pedestal and sending it across the room.

"There is no way Yvonne would do such a thing." Belinda grabbed her chest with one hand and put the other hand on the wall to steady herself.

Daryl hurried over and took her by the arm, guiding Belinda to the only seat in the room, an old armchair stuck in the corner.

"Get my medication." Belinda's chest heaved up and down. Daryl scurried off.

"I'm so sorry. Are you ill?" I asked, wanting to get down to what Bunny had told me about Belinda. I pulled the cookies from my cross-body, not really sure if this was a good time to offer them to her, but I knew in most cases, cookies were a good medication for calming the nerves.

She took one of the cookies and held it in her palm.

"I've had heart problems for a long time. When Ryan and Yvonne got married, they moved me in so I could be taken care of by Daryl." Slowly she shook her head. Her eyes were closed.

"I know what I told you is a shock, but she wanted you to know the hemlock she keeps in the greenhouse was confiscated for evidence." I'd made good on what Yvonne had asked me to promise to tell her mom.

She was definitely not taking the news well. Her cheeks flushed white, and her chest still heaved up and down at a rapid pace.

"Do I need to call your doctor?" I asked and knelt beside her.

"No." She opened her eyes and looked at me with a fear so deep that I could feel it. "I know she didn't do it. She doesn't have it in her. What about Jo Beth? She's the one who had the most motive to kill him for the company."

She took a bite, and her face relaxed.

"Not really. The company was already signed over to her, and Yvonne didn't disagree. She only wanted Ryan to mentor the child until he was educated or well trained. Ryan had no issue with that." I really wanted Jo Beth to have done it. "And Gio, the father, really had no reason to either."

Daryl, who came in with the medication, chimed in on the conversation. "He was bitter and angry over Ryan firing him. Gio said the accusations Ryan was making about buying the cheap meat would ruin his butcher career."

"That's true and looks like a great motive, only he got a much better deal than jail. Now his child will be heir to the company, and he didn't have to get his hands dirty at all. It's probably the ultimate revenge without killing anyone," I told them.

"I just can't believe it." Belinda looked at Daryl as if Daryl had some sort of answer. She ate the rest of the cookie. "You are really a good baker. I know Ryan and Yvonne enjoyed your coffee."

That wasn't the praise I was looking for when I offered my coffee and baked goods to people. What I wanted was the look on their faces and to see that coffee and cookies were a nice common denominator in any situation.

"Can you tell me about the greenhouse?" I asked Belinda when I noticed she was a little more calmed down.

"I don't know anything about it other than Yvonne complaining Ryan would rather be out there more than in here." Sadness and a worried look mixed on her face as the lines around her eyes and mouth deepened. "There's no way I could get out there, and I never saw Yvonne go either."

"Hello?" a woman's voice called from the front of the mansion. "Yvonne?"

"What is she doing here?" Daryl's head jerked up. "What are you doing here?" Daryl turned her question to the lady who walked into the room.

"Yvonne called me to meet her." The woman snarled at Daryl and took a moment to look at Belinda and me. "Hi, I'm Abigail Porter."

My eyes grew. *So, you're the best friend. The other woman.*

Why on earth would Yvonne ask Abigail to come see her if she knew she was going to confess?

CHAPTER FOURTEEN

"Where is Yvonne?" Abigail asked. By the annoying tone in her voice, she must have felt the same way Belinda felt about her.

"You have the nerve to waltz in this house after you've been dying to get in here as Ryan's wife, booting my sweet Yvonne out, and now you've driven her crazy to the point where she confessed to poisoning Ryan." The words seethed out of Belinda's mouth.

With shaky arms, she pushed herself up to stand out of the armchair. Slowly, with Daryl's help, she walked right over to Abigail and stood up to the mistress.

"Get out." Belinda pointed at the door. "You've ruined everyone's life, including a sweet innocent child that has yet to be born."

I stood there watching as the women seemed to remain still for a few seconds. Abigail's eyes were drawn down her nose as she glared at Belinda. Belinda lifted her chin with a pride on her face as she looked up at Abigail.

"Fine. I don't want to harm an old lady and make you die from a heart attack," Abigail said with a deceptive calm that unnerved me.

"I'll be right back," I told Daryl and Belinda, hurrying out of the room after Abigail.

Although Yvonne was now in the process of being locked up in jail, I still had unanswered questions that I needed to be answered for me to really accept that Yvonne had made that sudden confession.

"Abigail!" I called once I opened the front door. She was already getting in her SUV.

Her head jerked up, and her eyes slid over the roof of the vehicle and focused on me.

"I wanted to know if I could ask you a few questions." I walked down the front steps, taking care not to slip and fall.

The snow had now covered the ground. It was the type of soft snow good for making snowmen, and underneath that was the thin layer of ice that made it more treacherous than it looked.

"Who are you?" she asked. The fur coat she had on wasn't fake as I'd thought. I wondered if Ryan had given it to her, but I kept my mouth shut.

"I'm Roxanne Bloom. I own the Bean Hive Coffee Shop on the boardwalk." It was an automatic response I'd been giving people when I introduced myself. "Gosh. I'm sorry. I'm also a lawyer, and Yvonne had asked me to go with her for her questioning this morning—only I think she's confessed but didn't actually kill Ryan."

Abigail's shoulders fell. She appeared to have relaxed a little.

"I don't know what you want with me." She touched the handle of the door and jerked it open.

There were two men wearing green Carhart overhauls and green baseball caps with the Logsdon Landscaping logo on them. The men drove around on a golf cart. They both looked at us when they drove past and out into the field, stopping to check on some of the lights wrapped around one of the many light-up trees.

"Ryan loved Christmas." Abigail pinched her lips together like she let a confession slip.

"I know you're feeling a loss too." I let her know in a subtle way that I knew who exactly she was to Ryan. "I don't believe Yvonne killed Ryan. I think she's covering up for someone."

"You think I killed him?" Her eyes popped wide open, and her mouth dropped open a little.

"I didn't say that, but I know you were close with him, and I'd like to ask a few questions to just ease my mind and put my case to rest." I had nothing to hide, but I sure was going to go see Amy Logsdon so I could get a list of people from her company who'd worked at the Moores' mansion. Ears were everywhere, and I had to talk to everyone.

"Get in." She opened her car door and got in.

I opened the passenger side. The car was so warm and cozy inside with the big leather seats.

"You know, when Yvonne called me this morning, I thought she was going to forgive me." Abigail fiddled with the temperature controls. "Seat warmer?" she asked me.

"Yeah, that'd be great." I instantly felt a little warmth on my hiney when she pushed the button. This was a luxury I wasn't used to. "Forgive you?"

"Oh yeah. Ryan and I have been over for at least a year. It was a one-night stand thing. Not a big fling like all the people in Honey Springs made it seem like. We never made it to the bedroom either." I guess she noticed the confused look on my face because she continued speaking. "Like I said, Ryan loves—loved"—her voice cracked when she corrected herself—"Christmas. I have a ten-year-old son from a previous marriage, and Ryan and Yvonne throw these big Christmas parties. You know, the kind with Santa, gifts, food, cookies, and he even had reindeer flown in just for the occasion."

I'd never been invited. Those parties must've only been for the elite society of Honey Springs. *Loretta Bebe,* I thought and made a mental note to check with her when she came into the Bean Hive tomorrow morning since I was opening.

"A couple of years ago, both of us had a little too much to drink. We were standing in the kitchen talking, then all of a sudden, we kissed. Yvonne walked in, and she kicked me and my son out." Yvonne moved her gaze to look out of the windshield. "I've been trying to make up for it since. She blocked me from her phone, social media, parties. Even when my father died, I tried to contact her, but she never reached out. This morning was the first time I'd heard from her in two years."

"How did you hear about Ryan's death?" I asked.

"On the news. I was shocked and wondered if I'd heard right. Then I got on the computer and found an article about it. I wasn't in love with Ryan. It was a fluke kiss with drinking involved. That's all." She shook her head and looked over at me. "He died of hemlock poisoning?"

"Honestly, I'm not completely sure if it was that or drowning on top of it. But there was hemlock in his system. Enough to have made him have all the symptoms before he passed out and drove the truck into the lake." I left out the part about how I felt it was odd that Yvonne was an excellent swimmer and didn't even get herself out of the water, which made me think she did have a hand in the murder. Then my reasonable lawyer side replayed her sudden confession.

"I guess I just found it very odd how she had asked me to be present, and then she suddenly confessed after the sheriff told her it was hemlock poisoning and had photos from her social media of flower arrangements she had in her home, where she used hemlock as baby's breath." I honestly needed to get on social media. But more pressing things in my life took up my time, so I certainly didn't need another thing to add to it.

"Social?" Abigail laughed. "Yvonne is all about appearances. Even after Ryan and I begged her and pleaded with her, telling her the truth behind the kiss, she still didn't believe us. Saying how it made her look bad. Her social media was the same. Ryan is the one who would put the flower arrangements together. Yvonne never set foot in his greenhouse. He loved it out there. Yvonne would say that he had an obsession disorder. Once he got fixated on something, he did it until he got it or perfected it." She laughed. "It's how he got Yvonne. He chased her all over and wouldn't give her one moment's peace. Every time we were somewhere, he'd show up. After they got married, she'd say how he was obsessed with the butcher shop and spend his time there. When he got home, she said he was obsessed with the greenhouse and coming up with all sorts of hybrid plants like he did with meats at the butcher shop."

"So you're not surprised he had hemlock in the greenhouse?" I asked.

"Not at all. He grows things year around in that thing. Have you seen it? Top-of-the-line cooling and heating system." She looked past me and out the window. My eyes followed hers. "I'd say I'd show you, but I think they want me off the property."

Daryl and Belinda were standing at the front door of the house. Both women glared at the SUV.

"Would you like to stop by the coffee shop to continue our conversation? I have coffee and cookies." When I saw the smile cross her lips, I knew she'd be there.

"I can later today. Will you be there?" she asked when I was getting out of the car.

"Yes. I can." I shut the door and walked back up to say goodbye to Belinda. "I want you to know that I don't think Yvonne killed Ryan, and I'm going to get to the bottom of this."

"Thank you so much. But I don't want that woman anywhere near this house, even if we have to get a restraining order." Belinda gestured to the back of the SUV.

"I understand that." Then I went in for the kill. "But if she's the key to getting Yvonne off the hook for murder, then..." I shrugged.

"Daryl," Belinda gasped. "I bet you're right."

"Right about what?" I asked about the gasping and very shocked looks on their faces.

"Daryl said Abigail probably killed Ryan and made it look like Yvonne had done it." Belinda nudged Daryl, then waved us into the house as she vigorously ran her hands up and down her arms as though to ward off the chill.

"I just think that Abigail has tried to get her hands on Mr. Moore for a lot of these years. I see things, ya know." Daryl tapped her temples. "I'm 'sposed to be here takin' care of Miss Belinda, and I am, but it's like I blend in and no one even notices me."

"You overheard something?" I asked.

"Overheard nothing." Belinda gestured for Daryl to keep talking.

"Well, let's just say Mr. Moore and Abigail were seeing each other when they were telling Yvonne they weren't." What she just said meant that Abigail had flat-out lied to me. "This fall I was going out to find Mr. Moore in that greenhouse of his when it was late for Yvonne because we had to get Miss Belinda to the emergency room. I walked all the way to the greenhouse in the dark to tell Mr. Moore we had to go, and through the window, I saw something I shouldn't."

"Go on, tell her. She's going to help get Yvonne out of jail." Belinda nodded.

"Abigail and Mr. Moore were in the biggest lip-lock I'd ever seen, even in the movies." Daryl's eyes grew as a big sigh escaped her. "Yvonne came out lookin' for me. And that's when she saw it too."

"Well, you two let me handle this. I'm going to talk to her again, and I'm going to go see Yvonne." I heard my phone chirp the announcement of a text from inside the crossbody bag. "Yvonne needs to tell me why she confessed to a murder the three of us know she didn't do."

CHAPTER FIFTEEN

The text was from Aunt Maxi. She said she was going to stop by the Bean Hive before her lunch date to give me an update about what she'd found out from Pat, the busboy who'd spilled water all over Ryan the night of the wreck.

I wasn't sure I continued to think of the *wreck* as what had killed him, but calling it the night of his murder continued to put a sadness in my heart during what should be a joyous time of the year.

Speaking of joy, I still had so much I needed to do for the Christmas Day supper, but all the plans I'd made for that had been put on the back burner so I could focus on Yvonne.

"Bee's Knees Bakery and Wild and Whimsy to get those Christmas dishes I saw in the display window are probably two things I can do today," I rattled off a couple of the shops by thinking out loud the things on my to-do list. "Amy Logsdon."

I stopped at the end of the Moores' driveaway to make the call.

"Call Logsdon Landscaping," I said into my phone. "Is Amy Logsdon there?" I asked the person who answered and gave her my name when she asked for it.

"Hi, Roxy." Amy picked up with a cheerful voice. "Merry Christmas."

"Merry Christmas." This was one thing I did love about Honey

Springs. Every time you saw someone you'd not seen in a while, it was like no time had passed. "I have to say how magical you've made Honey Springs this year."

"You know, when the Moores asked us to decorate for them a couple of years ago and we ended up using one of our empty storage units, I knew this could be a very big business. Who has the space to store their decorations anymore? Plus, it seems like everyone is so busy, it's perfect we can do it." She laughed. "They go to work and come home to instant holiday fun without all the hassle."

"The Moores." I was glad she brought the subject up.

"Yeah. Tough, right?" She sighed. "I heard you and Patrick came upon the wreck and just can't believe Yvonne was arrested for his murder. I knew they had some pretty big fights, but from what my guys said, the making up was well worth the fight."

"I'm not so sure Yvonne killed him, and I'm representing her." I didn't tell the full truth, but that was okay. I was still curious about why Yvonne had taken the fall when I was almost sure she didn't poison Ryan. "I called because I wanted to see if I could talk to your employees who have been putting up the Moores' decorations. I'm trying to find out if they'd seen anything unusual or off outside of their fighting."

"Yeah. I have no problem. In fact, most of them are over at the nursing home putting the final touches on the banks before the big snowstorm comes. I think I've got two at the Moores' winterizing some things Ryan had put on the list." She told me something I'd not yet heard.

Those two employees must've been the two I'd seen on the golf cart.

"Did you say snowstorm?" I asked then put the car in drive. I surely didn't want to get stuck out here since I had to be at the coffee shop before Patrick got off work.

"You know how the weather reports around here go." She laughed again. "I'm sure they are probably wrong. Say, I'll get those names over to you, and you're more than welcome to head down to the lake and ask around."

"Thanks so much, Amy. Have a wonderful Christmas if I don't talk to you before." I hung up the phone. Then I reached over, flipped on the radio, and hummed to the smooth sounds of Bing Crosby's "White Christmas" along with a few other Christmas tunes while I drove my little car very slowly on the snow-covered roads all the way back to the boardwalk.

The snow didn't stop any of the tourists from getting to their holiday shopping. The carolers had found a nice spot under the awning at the Buzz In-and-Out diner.

"Happy holidays, Roxy!" James Farley, the owner of the diner, waved. "Santa Claus is coming to town!"

"You better keep the fact you're a great singer a secret because here comes Low-retta Bebe, and she just might recruit you for the town theater." I couldn't stop smiling because he made even more of a dramatic attempt to be louder when Low-retta walked up.

"Roxy, just the person I wanted to see. I was heading down to the coffee shop." Loretta's southern drawl turned "wanted" into "wouunted." She curled her leather-gloved hand in the bend of my elbow and waved at James over her shoulder, dragging me down the boardwalk.

"James, don't forget about the Christmas Day supper," I reminded him. He lifted his chin in the air for acknowledgement.

"I wouunted to let you know I'll be bringing my Twinkie cake to the supper." She squeezed my arm, but it was more of a painful pinch. "I can't tell you my recipe, so I wouuunted to let you know before you take a bite and get a hankering for any such idea about getting my secret family recipe."

"Oh, Loretta," I gasped and opened the door to the Bean Hive, letting her go first. "I'd *never* ask for such a prized possession," I assured her, though I could probably dissect the thing and figure out exactly what was in it, in which case I'd be sending her over the edge. Aunt Maxi would love that.

"Well. Well." Loretta tugged off the gloves in a dramatic one-finger way when she saw Aunt Maxi sitting at the bar at the front of the coffee shop. "I hear you've been making your rounds at the Moose."

"I hear they've got an opening just for you down at the crazy house." Aunt Maxi glared.

"Oh, Maxine." Loretta flung a glove Aunt Maxi's way. "What on earth do you wouunt with old Floyd? He can't barely walk, and he clearly has issues with eating. Every time I see the man down at the diner, he's always got something spilled on his shirt. And not to mention, you'd be stuck taking care of him."

"It's none of your business whose company I keep, Loretta." Aunt Maxi picked at the edges of her hair. "Besides, we are only having lunch."

"I have lunch with men all the time, but I don't get the rumors you're getting." Loretta pulled her phone from her purse. She jabbed at it a few times until she finally showed Aunt Maxi the screen. "You need to get on Compassion Companions."

"Compassion Companions?" Aunt Maxi and I asked in unison. Only, my voice was more of a "no she won't" and Aunt Maxi's voice was more of a "what is that?"

"It's a dating app that doesn't include men from the Moose. These are men who are well classed, if you know what I mean." Loretta gave a theatrical wink and a little grin. "They've got money. Not like Floyd and the ten-cent wing night at the Moose."

"Loretta." I took the attention off the app because I could see Aunt Maxi's wheels turning, which was never a good thing. "I appreciate you letting me know what you're bringing." I used my fingers to zip my lips. "I'll never ask for the recipe."

"Oh my Lord." Aunt Maxi returned to her regular self. "Are you bringing that Twinkie dessert?"

"It's cake," Loretta corrected her.

"It'd be much cheaper to head on down to the grocery store, grab a box of Twinkies, line them up, and frost the top." Aunt Maxi did all the hand gestures to convey the actions in her words.

"Forget I ever told you about Compassion Companions." Loretta shook a finger with a big diamond ring on it at Aunt Maxi. "You don't have enough class in your bones to even think about any men on there."

"Good gravy, Low-retta, who ever heard of someone getting all bent out of shape over a Twinkie?" Aunt Maxi only fueled Loretta even more. She stormed off and went over to grab a coffee from the coffee bar.

"Aunt Maxi, I'd be ashamed." I *tsk*ed and headed over to Loretta. "Coffee on me." I put my hand on her back. "And I can't wait to taste your famous cake."

"You must take after your mama's side." Loretta smiled and helped herself to two cups of coffee.

Bunny was too busy bringing out the chowder and breads for the soon-to-be lunch crowd to even care that Aunt Maxi was there, but when it was all put out and I'd cleaned off all the café tables and restocked the coffee and tea bar, I told her she could leave for the day. Her mood really took a dive when she saw Aunt Maxi in the coffee shop.

Aunt Maxi was still there, needing to talk to me, and waited patiently on the sofa stroking Pepper. They both sat there, enjoying the warmth of the fire.

I stopped briefly to look out the window. The snow was still falling. Honey Springs Lake looked like a glassy mirror with all the images of the snowy trees. The view was gorgeous, and I gave a little prayer for everyone to be safe while driving on the roads, even though the radio station mentioned on my drive back from the Moores' that the roads weren't slick. Amy had mentioned a snowstorm was coming, and from the looks of the flakes, I thought that just might be happening.

"Okay, what did you find out?" I asked Aunt Maxi and sat down next to Pepper.

"You were all wrong about Pat." Aunt Maxi took out her phone from her pocketbook. "This is Pat."

She handed me her phone, which showed a photo of Aunt Maxi and a woman with blond hair and big boobs spilling out of her white Watershed button-down.

"Are you having a shot?" I asked about the two small shot glasses they were holding up with big grins on their faces.

"Turns out Pat is a bartender who did work the night of the murder." Aunt Maxi took the phone and smiled. "I just so happened to be bellied up at the bar. What is it about bartenders that make you talk?"

"You mean liquor?" I knew it took Aunt Maxi only one small glass of wine to get a little tipsy. No wonder she was so mean to Loretta.

"I was a grown woman about to go on a lunch date. I needed a little relaxation." Aunt Maxi was sitting so close to me that I could smell her breath.

"Just how much relaxation did you drink?" I asked.

"That's not important." She grinned. The closer I looked at her, the more I realized Aunt Maxi was drunk. "What's important is that Pat is a woman and you were wrong, Roxanne Bloom." She jabbed me in the chest with her finger.

"I'm getting you a cup of coffee." I stood up and walked over to the coffee bar, where I got a big cup of black coffee. I set it down on the coffee table in front of the couch. "You drink that, and I'll be right back."

"Did you hear what I said?" She tried to make eye contact with me, but the liquor she'd been drinking had to be settling in because she was slurring her words. "They didn't have a busboy that night who was a boy."

"Okay." I shook my head at her and grabbed one of the blankets from the wooden ladder that was leaned up against the wall next to the fireplace, which was really there for decoration. She looked as if she were about to pass out. Clearly, she had no idea what she was saying.

"Let me know when Floyd gets here," she said and slinked down a little more into the cushions. She pulled the blanket up to her chin. Pepper wiggled his way underneath it, ready to take his nap too. "I told him to get me here."

"Mmmkay." I shook my head and made it back to the counter. "Aunt Maxi is drunk," I said to Bunny. "I asked her to do one thing: find out if Pat from the Watershed knew anything about the Moores when they were there the night of his death. And she goes, gets a photo with some bartender, and drinks."

"The bartender is Pat." Bunny untied her apron and shuffled over to the coat rack in exchange for her coat. "Pat is a woman. She sometimes fills in for Floyd at the Moose." Her voice drifted off as she pinned her little hat back on her head.

"Pat is a blond, very voluptuous woman?" I asked, realizing Aunt Maxi had been telling the truth in her drunken stupor.

"Very blond and very voluptuous." Bunny retrieved her black pocketbook from underneath the counter and hooked it on her arm. "Floyd said she was very good for business."

I could only imagine how that woman in Aunt Maxi's photo sweet-talked those older men into having more, just like she'd done to poor old Aunt Maxi, who was now sawing logs with her mouth wide open.

"So, there was no busboy in the night we were there?" I clearly remembered the busboy with the Watershed black shirt on, the logo on the right side of his chest. "Then who was that?"

I blinked a few times. The scene played in my head. Ryan and Yvonne were fighting. The busboy, or whoever he was, bumped into the table and spilled Ryan's water glass into Ryan's lap.

"Bunny," I gasped. "The guy at the Watershed. He gave Ryan a full glass of water to replace the one he purposely knocked over."

"Okay." She buttoned up her coat.

"No. Don't you know what this means?" I asked her.

"That Mr. Moore got soaked?" she questioned.

"No. The water was poisoned with the hemlock." It made perfect sense to me. "This guy doesn't work for the Watershed. I didn't notice him at any table but the Moores', and he didn't give anyone water but Ryan. Ryan drank it. There was enough time for it to get into his system before he started to feel the effects of it, which caused him to drive off the road and into the lake, where his lungs quickly filled up and he actually died from drowning."

I went to grab my phone to call Spencer Shepard, but when I heard Bunny gasp, I moved my attention back to her.

Floyd had walked into the coffee shop, and he was standing over an unconscious Aunt Maxi, who now had a wee bit of drool running out of the corner of her mouth.

CHAPTER SIXTEEN

"Let me get this straight." Crissy Lane had made herself comfortable in one of the café table chairs with all her fingernail polish laid out. She had her sun-washed blond hair pulled up into a ponytail, exposing the natural red roots below. Her red freckles were a dead giveaway she was a real redhead, but she didn't like her hair color for some reason. She blinked her big, long fake lashes as she tried to get clarity from me. "Maxine was passed out when Floyd came to pick her up for their lunch date, then he left with Bunny. Now they are back together?"

"Yep." I left out how I'd told Floyd that Aunt Maxi was a closet drunk and Bunny was a much better companion. Bunny didn't even correct me. She was so happy when Floyd apologized and asked her to go to lunch that she even made up more drunk stories about Aunt Maxi. I was sure Aunt Maxi would get wind of those tales and let Bunny have it.

"Maxine and Floyd have been all the gossip at the Honey Comb." Crissy Lane was probably my closest thing to a best friend, and she did hair and nails at the Honey Comb, the boardwalk's salon.

Like Patrick and I had, Crissy and I had hung out together during the summers I spent here and kept in touch like pen pals.

"They were starting to say they were either on Team Maxine or Team Bunny." Crissy laughed and looked around at the polish on the table, then she finally picked one. She shook it up, beat it on her palm, and shook it some more. "I'm so glad it's over. What did Maxi say when she woke up?"

"Patrick had stopped by for lunch, and I had him take her home." I walked over to the coffee bar and opened the cabinet on the bottom to refill the creamers, sugars, and stir sticks. "She was still pretty out of it."

The industrial coffee pots were brewing and ready for the afternoon employees, a couple of girls from the local high school who were in the business and home economics classes. I'd already mentored Emily Rich, who ended up becoming a pastry chef and opened the Bee's Knees Bakery, the bakery here on the boardwalk. Emily had gotten so busy now that she was baking all the cakes for the events for All About the Details, not to mention the special orders for all the holiday parties. I reminded myself to stop by there on my way home when the afternoon girls came because I did want to check on the fancy cookies I'd gotten for the Christmas Day supper.

My nephew, Timmy—Patrick's sister's little boy—loved Emily's sugar cookies. They had the right amount of icing, and her Christmas designs would make a perfect addition to the dessert table.

"I was thinking red with some candy canes painted for your nails." She showed me the very red polish. "And we can make your ring fingernail white."

Crissy was going to paint my nails for the festive occasion. Wearing nail polish was rare for me, since I was always keeping my hands in hot or soapy water. But I was willing to make her happy. After all, when she offered to do my nails, I had said no, but she ended up begging, saying it was my Christmas gift to her, which guilted me into it.

"One finger white?" I asked and looked over my shoulder when the bell over the door dinged.

"It's all the rage." Did Crissy really think I cared about popular things?

"Abigail," I greeted Abigail Porter when she walked in with her fancy fur. She'd changed her shoes from the boots I'd seen her in earlier to a pair of snow boots trimmed in fur. "Can I get you a coffee while we talk?"

"No. I'm fine." Her words were like daggers to my heart.

Who refused coffee? And how was I going to get her to open up about everything with nothing to keep our minds wondering... like coffee?

"I'll be done in a minute," I told Crissy.

Then when Abigail shooed Pepper away, I nearly wanted to kill her. I didn't trust anyone who didn't like all furry animals enough not to wear them.

"We can chat over here if you'd like." I suggested near the fireplace on the sofa where everyone loved.

"No. We can stand." She wasn't going to budge a bit. "Did you talk to Yvonne?"

"Not yet. I plan on going there after I get off work." I picked Pepper up, gave him a few kisses on his head, and then put him back down. That would hold him for a while, since he was bothering Abigail for a pat.

"Come here, Pepper." Crissy patted her leg. "Let's go get one of your treats," she told him and got up from the table, taking a nail polish with her and leaving Abigail and me alone in the coffee shop with only a few customers talking over scones and coffee.

"I do have something I need to ask you about since we spoke at the Moores'." I wasn't going to ease into it. I intended to rip it right off like a Band-Aid. "I understand that you'd been here recently to see Ryan in his greenhouse."

"Who told you that?" A look of horror crossed her face.

"It really doesn't matter, but from what I understand, you and Ryan were in a pretty big lip-lock." I didn't want to tell her too much.

She shifted from hip to hip and rolled her eyes with her jaw slightly open, and I could see her tongue playing with her teeth as if she were annoyed.

"Ryan called me a week ago." She sucked in a deep breath and shook her hair out, then flipped it so hard it landed over her shoulder. "He told me he wanted to tell me something in person. I was thinking he was going to tell me he and Yvonne had made amends about the truth between what had happened. He said he was in his greenhouse. I went there."

"How did no one see you park in the driveway? Or even get through the gated entrance?"

"There's another way onto the Moores' property down the road past the Hill Orchard."

"Really? No gate or anything?" I tried to think of exactly where the entrance would be, but nothing came to mind.

"Nope. There's a gravel drive that looks like it leads to nowhere a little past the Hill Orchard on the left." When she said gravel drive, I knew exactly the gravel drive she was talking about.

"I thought that was just a piece of gravel the transportation department had made for tourists who'd gone too far and needed to turn around." The winding roads were narrow, and I could barely turn my small car around for a U-turn, much less these bigger vehicles.

"No. It leads right to the greenhouse. Anyways, I went, and he told me how he and Yvonne had been having some issues. He even told me about Jo Beth and the baby. He also told me how he missed our friendship and my son." She brought her hand up to cough. She was shaking.

"I know it's hard to tell." I wanted her to relax and not be so nervous. "Let me get you a water."

I hurried through the coffee shop and around the counter to grab her a bottle of water. She took a few sips and then continued.

"Thank you. I guess I'm a little more upset about Ryan's death than I thought." She was a little paler than I'd remembered her from earlier. "I hate to say it, but it felt good hearing he missed us, and I kissed him."

"You did?" I wasn't sure I heard her right.

"Yes. He rejected me. He said that he didn't call me there to rehash what happened the year before but to tell me we weren't invited to the party and he didn't want me to hear it from anyone else." She swallowed hard and brought her hand up to her brow. "Anyways, Yvonne—

she loved him. The only reason I agreed to come here, though I'm feeling a little ill, is that I want to help in any way I can. I'm not sure why she'd be covering for someone, but now that you know what happened in the greenhouse, I can't help but wonder if he told her about the kiss, and she figured he'd been cheating on her like all the rumors out there said."

"Can you think of anyone who would want to kill him outside of the family?" I asked.

"He did take a phone call when I was there from Logsdon Landscaping." That got my attention.

"Logsdon?" I asked.

"They were in some sort of argument about the nursing home. He wanted something one way, and they did something different. He was mad." She shivered, pulling the edges of the fur coat up around her neck. "I really need to get going."

"Why would he care about the nursing home?" I asked her before she walked out.

"He owns it." Her words lingered along with the fancy perfume she wore as she darted out of the door.

"What was that about?" Crissy walked out of the swinging kitchen door.

"I'm not really sure, but I believe Yvonne Moore is covering up for someone. I can bet it's not Abigail Porter." I gnawed on Abigail's last words. "Did you know Ryan Moore owns the nursing home?"

"That's who Amy Logsdon was talking about when I was doing her nails last week. Something about how she'd given him a big break on their landscaping and the decorating over the past two years to help start the business, and he thanked them by starting his own landscape company in the spring. She was so mad and was trying to convince all the ladies under the dryer that they needed to stay with Logsdon Landscaping for all of their landscaping needs."

I could feel the shock contort on my face.

"What?" Crissy asked with a sideway glance.

"Did you hear her call him by name?" I needed to know.

"No, but I can find out." She pulled her phone out of her back pocket and started to type away. "I was busy running back and forth while she was talking, so I missed that part."

"You just gave me a perfect motive for Amy Logsdon to have killed Ryan Moore." I couldn't believe it.

"What?" Crissy's brows furrowed, and she looked at the phone when it beeped. "Yep. Ryan Moore." Whoever she'd asked had texted his name back.

"Jo Beth and Gio have been cleared!" I hollered over my shoulder on my way through the swinging kitchen door. I grabbed the whiteboard Aunt Maxi had started our little investigation on. I set it on the counter, and Crissy came behind it to look at the board.

"Last time we did this, you solved the murder." Crissy had once been involved in my nosiness, and we had all piled into her small VW to look for clues.

"And we are going to do it again." I pointed to the only three suspects we had. "Yvonne has now confessed, but I'm thinking she's covering for someone. Amy Logsdon has the most to lose. If she lost all her business to Ryan, she'd have nothing. When I asked her about him today, she was cool as a cucumber."

I could hear Amy laughing on the phone and in the next breath talk about Ryan's death, then laugh at something else.

"Taking away someone's livelihood is a pretty big motive." I wrote Amy's name on the whiteboard and put the dollar sign next to it for the motive. "And…" Slowly, I shifted my gaze to Crissy's face. "Amy would know all about hemlock."

Her jaw dropped open. We both turned to look at the door when the bell dinged. It was my afternoon employees. Pepper ran over to greet them.

"Oh my goodness, Pepper, you sure are festive with your red toenails." One of the girls squealed so loud she practically cut the air.

"What?" I jerked around to look at Crissy.

"I knew you weren't going to let me do yours, so while we were in the kitchen, I did his." Crissy shrugged and smiled.

. . .

"Oh, Pepper, I'm so sorry," I told him when we walked out of the door of the Bean Hive after I'd gotten the afternoon staff settled and sent Crissy on her way. "But you do look adorable with your matching red sweater on."

Pepper didn't care. He darted off down the pier instead of heading down the boardwalk.

"Pepper!" I yelled after him, knowing the pier and the Bait and Tackle Shop in the middle of it were closed. There was only one other set of footsteps in the snow, followed by Pepper's paw prints. "Where on earth is he going?"

The snow was falling, and I wanted to hurry up and stop by the Honey Springs Lake banks where Amy had told me the crew from the Moore house had been working. I knew I couldn't call Amy back and ask her about her little issue with Ryan, but I sure could play dumb and ask her workers if the rumor I'd heard was true.

Then I wanted to get home and out of the weather just in case it did turn into a snowstorm.

Luckily, Pepper had stopped right before the Bait and Tackle. He was digging in the snow drift that had gathered along the pier from the lake winds, which wasn't unusual when we did get snow.

"Pepper, stop that." I tried not to smile when I noticed his little red nails digging in the white fluffy snow. "It's probably a dead racoon," I told him when I saw some fur.

My mood faltered quickly when I saw him uncover what appeared to be boots trimmed in fur. He moved away. I bent down and uncovered what appeared to be a body.

"Abigail?" I gasped.

CHAPTER SEVENTEEN

At least I wasn't alone for what seemed like forever as I waited for Spencer Shepard to get there, because I wasn't sure what kind of shape I'd have been in if people hadn't heard me screaming.

Granted, it probably wasn't good for the community's businesses, since most of the people who had gathered around Abigail's body and me were more than likely tourists. I was sure a few of them had even called 911 because I could see them using their cell phones.

Spencer had moved Pepper and me back a few feet, where I joined the rest of the gathered crowd behind the police tape the deputies had put up.

"Why don't we all go to the Bean Hive?" I suggested to the crowd. "I own the coffee shop and can give free coffee and a sweet treat to warm everyone up."

The crowd started to disperse and walk down the pier towards the coffee shop.

"Please tell Spencer that he can find me at the Bean Hive," I told one of the deputies because I knew Spencer would be looking for me to answer some questions.

The Bean Hive was packed, and the afternoon employees were a little unsure of how to handle so many people, so I let the employees go home for the night. It was probably better since the snow was getting worse, and in no way did I want to put them in danger.

I had all the coffee pots going. I got all the burnt sugar cakes and ginger softies I'd made ahead of time out of the freezer and into the oven. If I'd not known better, I'd have thought I was having a little Christmas gathering with all the chatter and the smell of sugar, cinnamon, nutmeg, and freshly brewed coffee drifting all around us.

Pepper had retreated back into the kitchen, where he was safe and away from getting under people's feet, which he tended to do sometimes.

I grabbed a couple of logs from the big basket on the hearth and placed them in the fireplace, where I stoked them a couple of times to get a nice warm flame going. When my cell phone buzzed and I saw it was Patrick, I grabbed it to answer.

"What is going on down there?" he asked.

"I was leaving. I promise," I told him in a little preparation for what was about to come out of my mouth. "Pepper and I were leaving. Pepper ran down the boardwalk and uncovered a snow-covered and dead Abigail Porter."

"Abigail who?" Patrick didn't know who she was since I'd yet to tell him.

"Abigail was believed to be the woman having an affair with Ryan Moore, only she told me she wasn't. She's also best friends—*was* best friends," I corrected myself and pushed through the kitchen door when I heard the oven timers going off, "With Yvonne Moore until about a year ago."

"I want to say that I'm shocked you know all of this, but I'm not." The tone in Patrick's voice surprised me. He didn't seem all that upset. "I've got bigger issues here. Poor Maxi is sick to her stomach. I had to bring her here. The roads are getting bad."

As he told me about Aunt Maxi, I couldn't help but find it very entertaining, since Aunt Maxi never drank. I couldn't wait to get the real scoop but wasn't looking forward to telling her about Bunny and Floyd's reveal of their relationship either. Aunt Maxi's actions made it apparent she was somewhat lonely, or she'd not have been seeking Floyd.

I quickly got out the four sheets of treats I'd put in the oven and placed them on the cooling rack. Instead of plating them, I'd decided to push the cooling racks next to the coffee and tea stands so the guests could just help themselves.

I tucked my phone between my ear and shoulder while I maneuvered the contraption toward the door. Just as I was about to push through, Shepard stuck his head in.

"Hey, Patrick." I stopped and put the phone back up to my ear using my hand. "I've got to go. Spencer is here."

"I'm coming to get you in my truck, so don't leave. It's too dangerous." Patrick was always thinking of me, and no matter where he was in this crazy world, I knew he had my back and best interest at heart.

Spencer pushed the door open and pulled the cooling rack towards him.

"Just put it out on the shop floor near the coffee stand," I told him when I noticed everyone was getting coffee and not getting tea.

"What's going on?" Lesley Roarke was standing near the cash register with the bunny in her arms.

"Long story," I told her and took the bunny from her when she extended the animal my way. "Dead body on the pier, so I invited all the tourists who saw it in here for some hospitality so we didn't scare them away."

"Gosh." Lesley reached over and scratched the bunny on the head. "Jingle was a hit today. You were right about the kids loving her."

"Her?" I questioned. "Jingle?"

"The kids asked me her name, and I had no idea, so we came up with a name after we read the books chosen for story time. *Jingle the Festive Cat*, but we changed the name of the book to *Jingle the Festive Bunny* and adlibbed most of the book." Lesley smiled.

"You know, I love seeing you so happy." I ran a warm hand down her arm and tucked Jingle in my other one like a football. "Not that Jingle makes you happy, but you've embraced the Crooked Cat since your mom's passing."

"I really hated that bookstore growing up because it took mom away a lot. Book conferences, book sales, business conferences, and not to mention all the times she dragged me there." She shook her head. "Those were the events that I remembered when I was so bitter towards her. When I truly take the time to think back, it's the conversations she'd have with me during those long days in the bookstore that I didn't realize had shaped me into who I was until after she was gone..." Her voice trailed off.

"That's so amazing you have those memories and have let go of the hurt. Your mom would be so proud of you." I squeezed her arm before I let go.

"You think?" she asked as we stepped aside for someone to grab a ginger softie.

"I know." I ran my hand down Jingle. Her little nose twitched a couple of times, making Lesley and me giggle despite everything going on around us.

"You know..." Lesley grabbed Jingle back from me. "It's going to be so cold tonight. Why don't I get Jingle's cage and take her home with me for the night?"

"I think that's a great idea. Let me get her stuff." Since I'd yet to unpack anything Louise had left for her, I walked behind the counter and grabbed the bag with the adoption papers, food, hay, and treats, in hopes I wouldn't get those back.

"I grabbed a couple of cookies." Lesley shrugged, and I was happy to see she couldn't help herself.

"Can I talk to you now?" Spencer stepped in between us. "Lesley." He nodded.

"Spencer." She blushed and turned as if she didn't want me to notice.

Oh, I noticed.

"Sure. Can you help Lesley to her car with this stuff while I make sure everyone is good here?" Lesley didn't need help with a little bag and a cage, but her love life with Spencer needed a little push.

Though I knew Spencer wanted to protest because he was investigating and on the job, he was too much of a southern gentleman not to take up the challenge.

"Lesley, don't forget the Christmas Day dinner here. And I'm sure Spencer is coming too." I threw it in for good measure, not making eye contact with his searing stare before I pushed them out into the cold.

"Can I get you anything else?" I made my way around the coffee shop asking the various tourists but was happy to see they'd all helped themselves. A few of them had even placed some to-go orders. I quickly boxed those up and checked them out before Spencer made it back.

The coffee shop was clearing out, and I got Spencer a cup of cappuccino, his favorite, ready so we could talk about Abigail.

"There's a lot I need to tell you about this." I grabbed the whiteboard from behind the counter only to be met with a serious eyeroll from him. "You make fun of me, but this has been great." I didn't give him time to protest.

Conveniently, the last person left the coffee shop, leaving us alone. I took the opportunity to turn the sign around to Closed since it looked as if a big snowstorm would soon come down on Honey Springs, and the only people I saw on the boardwalk were the deputies still processing the scene.

"Y'all come in and warm up with some coffee and the fire when you need to!" I yelled out to them. They waved their hands and nodded.

"That's mighty nice of you, Roxy." Spencer pulled out his notebook. "You know the drill. Start from the beginning."

"First off, I have to say that if Abigail's preliminary autopsy report comes back with hemlock poisoning, I expect you to let Yvonne Moore go, because there's no way she poisoned Abigail from jail." I lifted a brow.

"Let's just take one thing at a time. We aren't sure how Abigail died, so we are treating it as such. Yes. We will do an autopsy." He somewhat agreed in his own way.

"Anyways..." I quickly recapped that Abigail had been Yvonne's best friend and that Yvonne caught her and Mr. Moore in a lip-lock at the

Moores' annual big Christmas party. I also told him how Abigail had gone to see Ryan in the greenhouse and kissed him. That might lead one to think Yvonne killed Ryan because of his philandering ways, but in reality, she could've done that a year ago, and now that Abigail was dead, there was no way she could've struck twice. "There's this busboy, but not a busboy from the night of Ryan's death."

"Now you have me all confused." Spencer had been writing so fast as I talked that he barely had time to take sips of his drink.

"The night of the murder, I noticed this busboy spilled Ryan's water glass all over him." I began to tell the story about this busboy who wasn't really a busboy. "So who was that guy?"

"I can get the security footage of the boardwalk from that night as well as the Watershed." Spencer plucked his phone off his utility belt and made a quick call while I helped a few of the deputies with some coffee when they walked in.

Patrick and Sassy had also come in, making Pepper so happy to see them. I was happy too.

"I'm almost done here." I kissed him when I noticed Spencer had gotten off the phone. "You can grab my stuff from behind the counter. I can come in early tomorrow to clean up and get ready for the half day."

Since it was Christmas Eve tomorrow, I would be open only a half day like the rest of the shops on the boardwalk. It was actually a day I looked forward to. Last year it'd been a quiet day, so the shop owners got together for a little festive cheer on the boardwalk. Big Bib brought up his portable firepit, and we had a great time around it.

He was the owner of the boat dock. It was still open during the winter months, which were actually his busiest, since he worked on people's boats and fixed any problems so they'd be ready to put in when boating season started back up.

"I can't help but think you need to question Amy Logsdon." It was something I knew would throw Spencer off. And I was right. The look on his face contorted into so many different forms of confusion that I had to force myself not to smile. "Apparently, Ryan Moore is starting a new business venture into landscaping."

I told him everything I'd heard and what Crissy Lane told me she overheard.

"You know they twist tales like the hair is twisted in that place," he said, reminding me how the gossip spread through the salon, but I didn't need reminding.

"Like my Aunt Maxi says, there's some truth to the tales. You just gotta weed it out." I shrugged. "Amy would have motive. This landscaping and now decorating is her life. She's put all her money in it. The Moores and the nursing home were her biggest customers."

"Nursing home?" Spencer looked up from his notebook.

"Ryan Moore bought the nursing home." I threw my hands up in the air as if to say, "Who knew?" I got up and grabbed my coat off the coat rack. "You let me know about Abigail's autopsy. I'd like Yvonne to go home before Christmas."

"Why would Yvonne confess if she didn't do it?" Spencer asked me a very good question that I'd been pondering.

"It's a very good question that I can't answer other than she's covering up for someone." I sucked in a deep breath and zipped up. "But who?"

CHAPTER EIGHTEEN

I'd like to say it was all festive and happy after Patrick took us home, but Aunt Maxi had passed out on the couch, leaving Patrick and me to retreat to the bedroom, where we brought a big bowl of popcorn with M&Ms in it. There, we watched a couple of Christmas movies we found on TV. So the night wasn't a total loss.

Even though I was the one who was going to open the Bean Hive, Bunny had texted me to let me know she wasn't coming in for the half day. She and Floyd weren't going to waste any more time. They were going to spend the day together, and she was sorry she wasn't going to make it on Christmas Day in light of what had happened. That meant she didn't want to be around Aunt Maxi, and I didn't blame her, though I did make sure she knew she and Floyd were more than welcome to come.

I got up before my alarm sounded and knew Patrick was fast asleep. Sassy snored between us with her big legs in the air. Pepper had found his way to the couch and snuggled up in the crease of Aunt Maxi's legs. He could stay home with them today while I worked.

Instead of risking waking them up, I pulled my hair into a ponytail and grabbed jeans and my Bean Hive sweatshirt. It would be a fine outfit for a half day. Besides, I had a lot of baking to do to get ready for tomorrow's big Christmas Day at the Bean Hive.

Patrick was off for the next week, so it was just fine that I took the truck to get me to the boardwalk through the snowstorm, which did hit overnight. Even though I could see the work crews had been plowing all night, they still barely made a dent.

With the truck in four-wheel drive, I was pulling into the parking lot in no time. The lights of Wild and Whimsy were on when I walked past. With my nose up to the glass window, I knocked on it with my gloved hand, getting Beverly "Bev" Teagarden's attention.

"Get in here." Bev rushed me into my favorite little shop.

I stepped inside. My eyes immediately looked at the set Christmas table Bev had decorated in such a lovely way, the one I'd been ogling from the outside for a couple of weeks now.

"I was wondering if you were going to be in today after all the big ruckus on the news."

"You mean the body?" I asked and ran my hand along the Christmas china on the display table I'd been eyeing.

"No, I mean Yvonne Moore being set free. She even complimented you, saying you gave her the best Christmas present ever—getting her free." She pointed at the small TV she kept on the counter that she watched during the day. "They just released her."

"What?" I couldn't believe it. "I had no idea she got out. That means Abigail was poisoned."

"What?" Now it was Bev's turn to be confused.

"Nothing. I need to go see Yvonne Moore." I turned my attention to the display window and gestured to the table. "Can you package these up for me? I want to buy the entire set. I think they are going to look great for tomorrow's lunch." I had to get over to the Moores' and see Yvonne before I opened. "Can Dan bring them down later?"

Dan was Bev's husband and business partner.

"We can make that happen." She winked.

"I've got to go, but I'll see you later today." I put my gloves back on. "Be sure to tell Melissa and Savannah to come too."

Melissa and Savannah were the Teagardens' daughters. They were very sweet young women.

I was never more thankful to have Patrick's truck and the ability to drive behind a snowplow than on my way to the Moores' house. The plow truck was taking a little too long. I wanted to go see Yvonne, get the details, and talk to her about Abigail and what her next move should be now that the sheriff seemed to have new leads.

I eased around the plow in the oncoming lane and kept my hands steady on the wheel even though I was using four-wheel drive. The big truck could just as easily slip on the road as any car. It was a few miles down the road, when I passed Hill Orchard, that I realized I'd gone too far. Luckily, the gravel turn-around wasn't too far, which I now knew was the drive to the back of the Moores' property where the greenhouse was located. I'd turn around and head back, certain not to miss the Moores' gated entrance.

The truck's headlights shined down the gravel path just as my curiosity kicked in. Like a force I couldn't control, an itch I had to scratch, I punched the gas, sending the truck right on down the gravel path until I stopped just shy of the greenhouse.

"Do I?" I asked myself and my conscience, not sure who was going to answer first. "Yes, you do."

I threw the truck in park and kept the headlights on for light since it was still too early for the sun to show itself. I closed my eyes and sucked in a deep breath.

"What are you doing?" I asked myself before I jumped out of the truck. "I've got to see for myself."

I was only doing something I would do anyway if I were trying the case in a court of law. But somehow someone was getting hemlock, and it was either coming from this greenhouse or Amy Logsdon's landscaping company, for which I was sure Spencer had gotten a warrant by now.

My legs pushed down deep into the snow, which practically came up to my knees. I trudged through, picking my legs up high in the air before letting them down, each step carefully maneuvered so I wouldn't fall and hurt myself. Especially when no one knew I was here.

I patted the pocket of my coat to make sure my cell phone was in there just in case I needed to call someone. When I made it to the greenhouse, I was glad there was a small roof overhang that'd kept the snow from forming underneath it. Just a small layer of fresh snow. A water drip came off the corner of the roof from where an icicle had formed and was starting to drip as the temperature began to warm a smidgen.

Carefully I turned the knob of the greenhouse door and opened it. The buzz of the heater and several plant lights filled the spooky air. I stepped inside and shut the door behind me. There were visible signs of the investigation as I walked down the one aisle of the greenhouse. Although I knew nothing about plants, I did know what a raid looked like, and I could tell from the aged, water-ringed spots that various plants had been moved around. The only types of plants being grown at the moment were various types of ferns. There didn't seem to be anything that resembled the hemlock photos I'd been looking at and reading up on in the books I'd gotten from Crooked Cat. And if they had been in there, I was sure Spencer had them moved to evidence.

With my curiosity satisfied, I headed back out of the greenhouse and stopped under the awning to zip up my coat so I could shield myself from the cold on my trek back to the truck. Then I noticed a shoeprint. One that had to been left since the snowfall and since the sheriff's department had been there.

I pulled my phone from my pocket and flipped the flashlight feature on to get a better look. It looked like a print from a tennis shoe and on the smaller side. Had the killer come back to get more hemlock? Did they find more hemlock here? Had Spencer not collected it all? Why would the killer have killed Abigail?

All these questions started to pop into my head. I only knew of one person who just might be willing to give me the answer.

Yvonne Moore.

Who was she covering up for?

CHAPTER NINETEEN

The truck's windshield was already covered with snow. It was coming down at a pretty good clip, and I knew if I didn't hurry up and talk to Yvonne, I'd not only have to wait until the roads were clear enough, but I wouldn't get the coffee shop open for any customer brave enough to get out in the snow.

"Can I help you?" Daryl asked from the speaker at the gate.

"Hi, Daryl. It's Roxy Bloom. I understand Yvonne is out…" I stopped talking as soon as I heard her buzz me in.

The lights on the trees lining the driveway were lit up, creating a magical scene with the snow on the ground. It was truly a spectacular winter wonderland, and if Yvonne did make it home to enjoy the scene one last time in the house, it would be bittersweet.

The snow globe blowup in the fountain was turned on and flooded me with memories of how my parents had kept the Christmas decorations on all day during Christmas Eve, all through the night, and all day on Christmas. That was when I knew Santa would come that night.

Daryl opened the door when I got out of the truck.

"Please take your shoes off." She pointed to the snow-covered boots. "Yvonne and Belinda are in the kitchen."

"Ho ho ho!" I did my best Santa impression and patted my belly when I followed Daryl into the kitchen. "I guess Santa came early for you," I told Yvonne.

The poor gal looked haggard. The big dark circles under her eyes told me she probably didn't sleep in jail, and her greasy hair told me she didn't shower.

"Roxy." There was a tone of relief in Yvonne's voice. She sat on one of three stools pushed up to the marble island. "I can't believe you stopped by in this crazy snowstorm. I had to beg one of the officers to take me home because I knew my mom couldn't drive."

"We really can't thank you enough." Belinda's face seemed less stressed. She grabbed the glass carafe from their coffee pot, grabbed a mug, and set it in front of me, at which point she filled it to the top with the brew. "You have to enjoy a cup of Christmas joy with us."

"I'd love to, but quickly." They had no idea how trained my esophagus was from all the years of brewing, testing, and remaking hot coffee I had under my belt. I was almost as much of a champion at coffee-brewing as Yvonne was at swimming.

I sat down on one of the stools and looked at the three-tiered display that was meant for food, but it appeared to be a catch-all for them, holding various envelopes, keys, and ink pens.

"You know you can get in trouble for interfering with a criminal investigation or even helping the killer if you are covering for someone," I blurted it out.

"I..." Yvonne looked taken aback by my sudden outburst.

"Listen, I have to know. Yvonne, you can't cover up a murder that's turned into a double homicide." It was not only illegal but immoral. "When you told Spencer you did it after we talked about the greenhouse, I knew you were lying. I recalled how you told me you hate being cold. I know you didn't walk to the greenhouse in your bare feet because you don't wear anything but heels. And you told me Ryan had hired Logsdon because you hated gardening. You lied. You lied to Sheriff Spencer about everything."

Belinda and Daryl looked back and forth between Yvonne and me.

"I thought maybe Abigail did it." She shook her head. "Not that I didn't want to bring Ryan's killer to justice, but I do love Abigail despite what happened between us. I'm probably more upset she's dead than Ryan only because I know that Ryan was the one who came on to her. I know she turned him down, but the second time, in the greenhouse, she was vulnerable and lost. If Ryan had not tried to kiss her in our kitchen a year ago, she'd never have tried to kiss him in the greenhouse."

How did she know about the greenhouse? My oh-crap-on-a-cracker meter started to tick. Had I been wrong all along? Did Yvonne really kill him?

I slid my eyes past the door frame and into the big family room. I could see the empty bookshelves where Yvonne's prized swimming trophies used to be proudly displayed.

"There is one thing that did disturb me about the night Patrick pulled you out of the water." I glanced back around to look at her feet. They were nicely manicured and small. Did the shoe print in the snow at the greenhouse just so happen to be hers? Did she really not own a pair of tennis shoes? "I had no idea you were a champion swimmer until I came here and your mom was putting your trophies in a box."

"Yvonne is home now." Belinda spoke up. "I don't like your line of questioning. You make it sound like you believe Yvonne did kill Ryan. How do you know Abigail didn't do it and then poison herself when she knew the police were getting closer to her as the murderer?"

"Good point." I could feel the air in the room get a little thicker and less... well... filled with Christmas cheer. "She has a young son. I spoke to her maybe within the hour of her death, and she sure didn't seem like she was in any mood to kill herself, though she said she felt ill."

"It's fine, Mom." Yvonne shifted in her chair to look at me. "What does me being a good swimmer have to do with anything?"

"I'm not sure why you didn't swim to the top. Maybe the amount of time it took Patrick to get you out and up on the banks would've been enough time to save Ryan. Unless you didn't want Ryan saved. Or even yourself." I stared at Yvonne. "Yvonne, did you slip Ryan the hemlock? Did you plan on not surviving a crash that night as well?"

"That is about enough." Belinda smacked her hand on the counter so hard that it got my attention. "I won't have this in my house. Get out!"

Yvonne sat completely still and kept my stare. She didn't flinch or budge. That was my cue that I better get out of there.

Slowly I got up, and when I turned around to go back to the front door, I noticed a pair of tennis shoes tossed on the drying mat next to the back door. One was placed on its side with the sole facing out.

"That shoe looks a lot like the shoeprint I took at the greenhouse this morning. And small like your feet, Yvonne." I pulled my phone out of my pocket and swiped to my photos, showing the photo face out.

"This is ridiculous." Belinda walked over to me faster than I'd ever seen her walk in the past few days. She pinched my arm in her grasp, pushing me toward the entrance of the house. "If you won't leave on your own, I'll be more than happy to help you."

"Ouch." I jerked my arm away from her and smacked over the three-tiered stand, sending it crashing to the floor and spilling out the contents.

"I'm sorry. I didn't mean to press any buttons." I bent down and gathered as many things as I could. "But I just can't wrap my head around why you'd confess. It's the lawyer in me."

I put the items on the marble island and noticed the nursing home pamphlet was one of them. It was creased opened to an image of a one-person room with a big red ink circle around it and Belinda's name accompanied by several explanation points.

"Belinda." I gasped and looked at her, then down at her feet. "Of course." I started that nervous laughing thing I did when I knew I was in a pickle. "Yvonne has your feet. You wear tennis shoes. You can walk pretty well. And Ryan wanted to put you in the nursing home. You poisoned him, but how did you do it?"

"I told Yvonne you were trouble," Belinda spat, her little-old-woman ways suddenly disappearing.

"Mom, please don't." Yvonne covered her ears. "I don't want to hear it."

"You're going to hear it, and we are going to get rid of her unless you do want to go to jail for knowing deep down that I did kill Ryan. And it was all for you." Did Belinda just really confess to killing Ryan?

"Belinda!" Daryl hurried to her side. "I don't think you know what you're talking about. We need to get you medication."

"Of course I know. You're the one who gave that young boy money and extra hemlock the night they went out to dinner. Don't be acting like this is all my fault, Daryl."

"What young boy?" Yvonne asked with a panic in her voice.

"The young man that works for the landscape company. He needed extra money. He said he was only hired for holiday work. The Logsdon Landscaping Company was worried about being able to stay open because Ryan was going to run them out of business," Belinda snarled. "He was ruining everyone's life. He didn't care who he hurt. He cheated on you. He never was a father to Jo Beth, and he fired Gio for no reason whatsoever. He was going to take away all the livelihood the Logsdons had, and then you'd be here with nothing." She shook a finger at her daughter. "You were going to let him put me in that nursing home. I heard him telling you that the two of you were going to move and stick me in there alone. With no one."

"You mean to tell me you killed Ryan because he mentioned a nursing home and your name in the same sentence?" Yvonne walked over and stood nose to nose with the woman who had brought her into this world. "When Shepard said they'd found hemlock in the greenhouse and Ryan was poisoned with hemlock, I knew it had to be you that killed him. I was willing to take the fall for you, but when they let me go because Abigail had been killed the same way, I thought I got it wrong because you loved her. You have been begging me for the past twelve months to mend our friendship."

"I was until she came back here yesterday after I kicked her out. She figured it out. She came back here to tell me how she knew I was connected somehow while she sipped on some of my freshly brewed coffee." Belinda looked at me. "Was your coffee good?"

My heart sank. Did she really just let me know that she *poisoned* me? Instantly I felt sick.

"You hold on right there." Yvonne pointed at me to tell me to stay, and she grabbed her phone. "Yes. Please send an ambulance and the sheriff to the Ryan Moore home. This is Yvonne Moore, and my mother killed my husband and Abigail Porter."

CHAPTER TWENTY

"I was dreaming of a white Christmas, but I never figured it'd be this white." I had decided to pull my hair up in a bun and wear a black turtleneck and buffalo check A-frame skirt along with a pair of heels for the Christmas Day dinner. Most of my friends and family had only seen me wear the staple outfit, jeans or khakis with a Bean Hive logo shirt, which I covered up with an apron that had more spills on it than one could count.

"I'm just glad I'm spending another Christmas with you." Patrick was putting the final cloth napkins around the table in the coffee shop. "Glad you didn't test positive for hemlock poisoning."

"That was a scare." I sucked in a deep breath and continued to look out the window with a grateful outlook given how this time yesterday had turned out.

Yvonne had done the right thing and called 911. After they got there, the ambulance had whisked me off to the hospital, where they did all sorts of tests to make sure I wasn't poisoned. After Spencer heard I'd gotten the all clear, he was in my room lickety-split.

He told me they were on the cusp of pinning either Belinda or Daryl as the killer. Spencer had taken my leads about the busboy and gotten the video footage like he said he would do, and it revealed that the young man did work for the Logsdon Landscaping Company. Of course, Amy Logsdon had come out in the clear with my theory.

Then there was Abigail. He said he'd not put the puzzle pieces together until they'd used her cell phone. Shepard found phone pings from various cell towers where Abigail had been to see Belinda a second time that day after I'd seen her there. Phone records showed a call placed from the Moores' home to Abigail's phone, leading him to believe the killer was in the house and not Yvonne, because she was locked up.

"Hey buddy." Pepper sniffing my ankles brought me out of my thoughts. "You want to help me get the turkey out of the oven?"

I twirled around on the toes of my high-heeled shoes and headed to the kitchen. I took in all the beautiful details of what Patrick and I had created for our family and friends.

We had moved all the café tables to the side and formed a big U-shape constructed of three large tables we'd gotten from All About the Details. The Teagardens had brought down the table settings and placed them in front of each chair along with cloth napkins and poinsettias neatly used as centerpieces. The Christmas tree was lit next to the roaring fire.

But it was the turkey and all the baked goods that made it feel and smell like Christmas.

"That looks good," I told Pepper and Sassy when we pulled open the oven door and looked at the golden bird. "Stand back." I grabbed two potholders and pulled the big bird out, carrying it to the swinging door and backing out of it, where I found we'd gotten guests.

Yvonne Moore was there with Jo Beth and Gio. Boy, was I surprised.

"I'm so glad to see you." I didn't invite them, but we had plenty of food. "Please help yourself to something while we wait for everyone to come."

I pointed them to the snack table.

"We can't impose." Yvonne waved a hand. "We wanted to stop by and thank you. It seems you've done more for our little family than you could know."

"You aren't imposing." I insisted they stay. "We are all family and friends here."

"Are you sure?" Gio asked.

"Man, we are more than sure." Patrick had come over with the carving knife in his hand. "In fact, I'll let you do the honors since you're the real butcher around here."

"All right." Gio nodded, and off he and Patrick went.

"You don't need to thank me for anything." I put my hand on Yvonne. "I'm really sorry for your losses." My statement even included her own mother, who I knew was a big loss from her life, as were her best friend and husband.

One by one, all the people we loved came in from the snow and warmed by the fire. Once people stopped dribbling in, we decided it was time for prayer and food.

Patrick and I moved three of the chairs that I'd figured to be Bunny Bowoski's, Loretta Bebe's, and Floyd's if Bunny decided to bring him. They'd not showed.

We passed the food around. I was happy to see Aunt Maxi had recovered from her day-drinking experience and seemed to be much hungrier than normal. She even sat next to Mom. All the shop owners had come, and we were all talking when the bell over the coffee shop dinged. All the chatter stopped when we saw Bunny and Floyd standing there. My eyes shifted to Aunt Maxi.

I watched with bated breath, hoping she'd not say anything, but that was too much to ask for.

The sound of the chair legs scooting across the tile floor when Aunt Maxi scooted it away from the table cut the silence.

"We saved you two a seat. Roxy?" Aunt Maxi looked at me, giving me the eye to get the chairs back in place.

"Yes." I jumped up. "We didn't think you were coming, so we put them back."

I played along with Aunt Maxi's lie, one I could totally get my heart into.

"I've got it." Patrick grabbed my hand and stood up. "Sit. I've got it." He kissed me and pushed my chair back in for me when I sat down.

I took a deep sigh of relief. Patrick quickly got a couple of more chairs. Aunt Maxi grabbed a few more of the place settings I'd bought from Wild and Whimsy while everyone scooted around the big table to make room.

Once everyone was situated, the conversation began and filled the room with laughter, tales, and sheer love.

"Here, pass the green beans down to Floyd." I picked up the bowl and handed it to Patrick. Like an assembly line, we passed the food down to the happy couple.

Aunt Maxi winked.

There was definitely something about the spirit of Christmas that brought the unlikeliest of conflicts to an end… even if that meant a truce just for one day.

THE END

If you enjoyed reading this book as much as I enjoyed writing it then be sure to return to the Amazon page and leave a review.

Go to Tonyakappes.com for a full reading order of my novels and while there join my newsletter. You can also find links to Facebook, Instagram and Goodreads.

Keep reading for a sneak peek of the next book in the series. Dead To The Last Drop is now available to purchase on Amazon.

Chapter One of Book Eight
Dead To The Last Drop

I liked nothing better than the smell of the freshly made coffees that brewed in the industrial coffee makers. The rich scent of my very own Peruvian roast curled around me like a warm blanket, and Pepper lay at my feet, warming them with his body heat.

Who knew how much a sweet Schnauzer could warm not only my feet but my heart? I reached down and patted him on his sleepy head, but he didn't move. The fireplace glowed with an orange flame and heated the Bean Hive to a perfect temperature for the customers who would arrive when we opened.

The coffee makers beeped to let me know the coffee had been fully brewed, sounding like a wonderful melody. The sound was music to my ears and a signal to get up off the couch and put the breakfast treats in the oven so they'd be hot, fresh, and ready for anyone who needed a little sweet with their morning coffee.

Pepper lifted his head to see what I was doing. "I better get those in the oven," I told him. "It's still coming down pretty good out there."

The entire front of the Bean Hive consisted of windows with a long counter-type bar in front of them. Behind the long bar stood stools for the customers who wanted to enjoy their coffee while taking in the magnificent view of Lake Honey Springs, the actual reason why Honey Springs, Kentucky, was a tourist town. Even in the winter.

"So pretty," I said with a sigh as I looked out at the freshly fallen snow down the pier and across the boardwalk. Then I turned to head back toward the kitchen of my coffee shop.

Bunny Bowowski, my only full-time employee, would be here soon. We took turns opening, and today was my day, which I didn't mind. I'd left my husband, Patrick, and our poodle, Sassy, at home and fast asleep, tucked into the warm bed.

After I went to Pet Palace, our local no-kill shelter version of the SPCA, Pepper had adopted me as his human, and Sassy and Patrick came along later. That reminded me to keep my ears peeled for Louise Carlton, owner of Pet Palace. She said she had a new cat for me to showcase at the Bean Hive this week.

I had gone through a lot of hoops to get the health department to even agree to let me showcase an animal from Pet Palace. Everyone deserved a loving home, and having an animal that needed a home here during the week was a perfect way for people to see how the animal acted and how they might fit together with that animal. I was proud to have been able to help all the animals I'd had in the coffee shop. They were all adopted out and living their best lives.

Louise had already told me a little about the sweet feline, so I was excited to get her into the shop to give her some good loving. It was still a little too early for Louise to show up, but you never knew whether someone was going to be early or not. I certainly didn't want her waiting outside in the snow with the cat.

I dragged the coat rack sitting next to the counter and used the rack to prop open the swinging door connected to the coffee shop and the kitchen just so I could hear if anyone was knocking.

The Bean Hive opened at six a.m. during the week and a little later on the weekends. There wasn't an exact time I opened, but six a.m. was when we got up and moved around. During the winter months I didn't open on Sundays, but I did come in to order and prepare the food for the upcoming week.

We were technically a coffee shop, but I liked to make everyone feel welcome and at home. Coffee was great for that, but a little something for the belly was also good. Each week on the menu I had a breakfast item outside of the usual donuts, scones, and muffins. I provided something like a quiche or breakfast-type casserole with a little more oomph for the hungrier customers. I offered a light lunch as well. These food items were the exact same for a week, so I made them in bulk on Sunday.

The kitchen had a big workstation in the middle where I could mix, stir, add, cut, or do whatever I needed to do to get all the recipes made. Someone might look at it and call it a big kitchen island, but it was where all the magic happened. There was a huge walk-in freezer as well as a big refrigerator. I had several shelving units that held all the dry ingredients and a big pantry that stored many of the bags of coffee beans I'd ordered from all over the world. I liked to roast my own beans and make my own combinations, but the coffee shop had pretty much reached its capacity of what I could roast, and the small roaster was in much need of a bigger upgrade. However, I rented the space from my aunt Maxine Bloom, and there was no room to expand on the boardwalk where we were located. On my right was the Queen for the Day spa, and to the left of me was Knick Knacks, a little boutique store with a variety of items. Aunt Maxi didn't own those, so expanding was pretty much out of the question because they weren't going anywhere anytime soon.

Quickly I put the muffin tins in the oven to get them heated up and ready to put in the glass display counter. Then I grabbed the dry ingredients I needed to make the coffee soufflé, which would sell out so fast. Every time I made it, it was a hit. Of course it was amazing. Who didn't like sugar, vanilla, and coffee?

"One envelope unflavored gelatin, sugar, salt and vanilla," I said to myself, plucking the items off the shelf as I found them. "Now for a little brewed coffee." I grabbed the carafe out of the small pot of coffee I kept in the kitchen for me and put it on the workstation with the dry ingredients. Then I went to the refrigerator to grab the milk and eggs.

Eggs didn't really need to be refrigerated, but for some reason I refrigerated them. Everything in the coffee shop was prepared with the freshest of ingredients. If I could get it locally, I did. My honey came from the honey farm across the lake from the boardwalk. The vegetables and eggs came from Hill's Orchard, and the coffee beans came from all over the world.

"Hi do!" From the coffee shop, I heard the familiar greeting from my Aunt Maxi. "It's me! Maxi!" she called out like I didn't recognize her voice.

But I knew she did it to let me know she wasn't some random

burglar. Aunt Maxi owned the building where my coffee shop was located, and she had a key. She showed up whenever she wanted.

"Back here!" I hollered back just as I finished pouring the soufflé into a serving dish and putting it into the chiller to set. I had already made some earlier this morning, so I took those out of the chiller and was pleased with how they turned out.

"Oh, coffee soufflé today?" Aunt Maxi walked into the kitchen. She wore a bright-red wool coat with big purple buttons.

"Yes." I couldn't stop from smiling when I saw her.

She also wore a pair of snow boots with her polyester brown pants tucked in. She tugged off the purple knit cap that matched the color of her hair.

"What?" She used the tips of her fingers to lift her already-high hair in place.

"Your hair. I don't think I've ever seen it that purple." I walked over and kissed her.

"Honey, it's a new year. New me." She unbuttoned her coat and hung it up on the coat rack that continued to prop the kitchen door open. Her patchwork hobo bag hung across her body. She dug down deep in it to retrieve a big can of hair spray.

"Seriously?" I asked. "My food," I reminded her, but it didn't stop her from spraying.

"I've got an image to keep up now that I'm in the new play." And that was why she was here.

"Play?" I took the bait to hear all about her new adventure.

Aunt Maxi was always getting into something. I always enjoyed hearing about them even if not all of them had come to be. She was the reason I moved to Honey Springs after my divorce.

Aunt Maxi had always lived here, and when I was a little girl, my father would come to visit, bringing me with him. I loved being here so much I even started to spend my summers here. It wasn't until I'd gone off to college, earned my law degree, gotten married to another lawyer, and opened a law firm with my spouse that I realized our client policy was to help all our clients in more than just law.

Well… that was when I found my now-ex-husband, Kirk, doing counseling than was more than verbal, if you knew what I meant. It was then that I ran off into the arms of my aunt, who just so happened to have this space open while Honey Springs was in desperate need of a coffee shop.

I was still a lawyer and kept my license up. Good thing, too, because I give out so much advice around here that I find it soothes my lawyer side. But coffee was my passion. I loved all things surrounding coffee, and gathering with friends for a little gossip just might be my favorite thing of all. Gossip happened all day long at the Bean Hive. So technically, working here didn't feel like work to me.

"Mmmhhhh. Didn't you notice the new dowel rod flags on the lights around town?" she asked.

Aunt Maxi was referring to the dowel rods on the carriage lights that were all over Honey Springs and the boardwalk. Every season or occasion, the beautification committee had special flags to hang on the rods. It was a special touch to add to our small southern lake town.

"Well, I want you to know that Bunny Bowowski didn't vote for them, and neither did Mae Belle Donovan." She shrugged and curled her nose in disgust. "Low-retta Bebe is the producer of this year's local theater."

Aunt Maxi didn't have to say any more than that. I knew this conversation would need a cup of coffee.

"Grab those muffins and the stack of cookies," I told her. I grabbed the soufflés and the serving tray of mini breakfast quiches I'd made. The pastries were all ready to go in the display case "While we fill the display case, you can tell me all about it."

When both of us were through the door, I put down the items in my hand and moved the coat tree back. Turning back around to look at the inside of the coffee shop, I gasped at the beauty of the coffee shop.

"I'll tell you after I go to the bathroom." Aunt Maxi headed there.

Even though Aunt Maxi owned the building, she didn't give me a cut on the rent. I didn't expect her to since it was part of her income. Rent was a little steep, but I'd watched a few DIY videos on YouTube to figure out how to make the necessary repairs for inspection when I first decided to open the coffee shop. I couldn't've been more pleased with the shiplap wall, which I'd created myself out of plywood and painted white so it would look like real shiplap.

Instead of investing in a fancy menu or even menu boards that attached to the wall, I'd bought four large chalkboards that hung down from the ceiling over the L-shaped glass countertop.

The first chalkboard menu hung over the pie counter and listed the pies and cookies with their prices. The second menu hung over the tortes and quiches. The third menu over the L-shaped counter curved listed the breakfast casseroles and drinks. Above the other counter, the chalkboard listed lunch options, including soups, as well as catering information.

On each side of the counter was a drink stand. One was a coffee bar with six industrial thermoses containing different blends of my specialty coffees as well as one filled with a decaffeinated blend, even though I never clearly understood the concept of that. But Aunt Maxi made sure I understood some people drank only the unleaded stuff. The coffee bar had everything you needed to take a coffee with you, even an honor system that let you pay and go.

The drink bar on the opposite end of the counter was a tea bar. Hot tea, cold tea. There was a nice selection of gourmet teas and loose-leaf teas along with cold teas. I'd even gotten a few antique tea pots from the Wild and Whimsy Antique Shop, which happened to be the first shop on the boardwalk. If a customer came in and wanted a pot of hot tea, I could fix it for them, or they could fix their own to their taste.

A few café tables dotted the inside, as did two long window tables that had stools butted up to them on each side of the front door. It was a perfect spot to sit, enjoy the beautiful Lake Honey Springs, and sip on your favorite beverage. It was actually my favorite spot, and today would be a gorgeous view of the frozen lake with all the fresh snow lying on top.

"Burrrrr. It's cold." Bunny Bowowski walked through the door, flipping the sign to Open. "Me and Floyd enjoyed your soufflé so much last night." She loved talking about her new relationship with Floyd.

Bunny's little brown coat had great big buttons up the front, and her pillbox hat matched it perfectly. The brown pocketbook hung from the crease of her arm and swung back and forth as she made her way back to the coffee bar. There, she'd grab a coffee before she hung up her coat and put on her apron.

"Did you notice the new lamppost flags?" she asked and waddled back over to the coat tree. Slowly she unbuttoned her coat and hung her purse and her coat on the coat tree. The sound of the water running in the bathroom caught her attention. "What was that?"

"Aunt Maxi is here, so maybe you shouldn't talk about the flags," I suggested, since they were probably talking about the same thing and clearly on opposite sides of whatever it was they spoke of. If it was no big deal to either of them, neither would've brought it up.

"Good thing she's here. I'm gonna give her a piece of my mind." Bunny brought the mug up to take a sip.

"Were you flapping your lips about me?" Aunt Maxi stood, glaring at Bunny with her fists on her hips. Her purple hair glistened in the light of the coffee shop.

"What are you doing here so early?" Bunny gave Aunt Maxi the once-over. "You trying to get to Roxy before me, huh?"

"Listen, we are open, and I don't have time for all of this." I looked between the two of them.

"Did you not see that snow out there?" Bunny asked. "It took Floyd almost an hour to get me here."

"It takes Floyd an hour to get anywhere without snow," Aunt Maxi muttered under her breath but knew Bunny could hear her.

"Ladies," I said in my warning tone, though I knew it wasn't going to work. "Everyone grab a cup of coffee, and let's talk about what is going on."

Bunny already had her cup and sat down at the café table nearest her. Aunt Maxi sat down at a different table near her. Instead of trying to get them to compromise at a neutral table, I simply let them stay, grabbed Aunt Maxi and myself a cup of coffee each, and stood so I could address them both.

"What are the flags about?" I asked Aunt Maxi, who was busy doctoring up her coffee with creamer and sugar. My eyebrow lifted as I wondered why she even bothered having coffee in the cup.

"They are about the play." She lifted her chin in the air and looked down her nose at Bunny. "Bunny and Mae Belle are mad because they didn't get an offer to be in the play, as I did."

"We don't care one iota about that, Maxine," Bunny chimed in. "We want to use the flags we had last year to promote all of Honey Springs for the winter instead of spending money on new flags when we could use that money somewhere else."

Bunny had a good point, but I didn't dare tell Aunt Maxi. She'd have a conniption right then and there. It wouldn't be a pretty sight.

"What good is doing a play for the tourists if they don't know about it?" Aunt Maxi snapped back. "We could put it in the paper, but tourists don't buy our local paper. We could put it on flyers in the shops, but look at that snow. Who is going to come out in the snow right now?"

Then I could see Aunt Maxi's point.

"Roxanne." When Aunt Maxi said my full name, I knew she truly believed what she was about to say. "I'm telling you, when Bunny thought she had a shot at the lead of Vi Beauregard, she was all over using whatever funds to promote it. Even had the boys at the Moose talking about what a good Vi she'd be."

"Why," Bunny said with a gasp, "I can't help it if the boys at the Moose like me over you, Maxine Bloom. I guess my niceness trumps your gaudiness." Bunny's eyes drew up and down Aunt Maxi until they fixed right up on Aunt Maxi's purple hair.

Aunt Maxi looked like one of those pressure cookers. I could feel her anger curling up from her toes and straight up to her hair. I swear, I thought I saw her hair stand up even more on its own.

"Why, Bunny Bowowski!" Aunt Maxi smacked the table so hard that when she got up, it almost tumbled over. "How dare you talk to me like that!"

Just as I was about to make sure Aunt Maxi wouldn't leap across her table to try to get to Bunny's throat, the bell over the door dinged.

"Welcome to the Bean Hive." Bunny's disposition turned on a dime. She planted a big smile on her face and stood up. Just as pleased as a peach, which I was sure was because she'd gotten the last word in.

She and Aunt Maxi knew I wouldn't stand for their bickering while there was a customer.

Dead To The Last Drop is now available to purchase on Amazon.

RECIPES FROM THE BEAN HIVE

Burnt Sugar Cake
Gingerbread Softies
Twinkie Cake
Rich Potato Chowder

Burnt Sugar Cake

Submitted by Jeannie Daniel

This is an old-family, old-fashioned recipe.

Burn ½ cup sugar in a heavy skillet, carefully add ½ cup boiling water and boil until it is syrupy.

Sift together 1 ½ cups sugar, 1 teaspoon salt, 3 cups flour.

Dissolve 1 teaspoon of baking soda in a little warm water in a 1 cup measuring cup and then fill the rest of the way up with cold water.

Cream ¾ cup butter with 1 teaspoon vanilla.

Add 2 eggs and beat smooth.

Stir in the syrup mixture then beat in dry ingredients alternately with dissolved baking soda.

Bake in an 8 or 9 inch pan 30 to 35 minutes at 350 degrees

Gingerbread Softies

Submitted by Sharon Rust

Ingredients

- 1-18.25-oz box spice cake mix
- 1-8oz pack cream cheese
- softened ¼ cup (½ stick) butter melted
- 1 large egg
- ¼ cup packed Brown sugar
- 2 teaspoon ground ginger
- 1 teaspoon cinnamon
- 2 teaspoon vanilla

Directions

1. Take about ½ of cake mix and blend with the other ingredients until smooth then add remaining cake mix. (you might have to do the remaining cake mix with spoon unless your mixer is strong)
2. place by teaspoon full about 2 inches apart on prepared cookie sheet.
3. Bake 10-13 minutes in 350 degrees oven.

Twinkie Cake

Submitted by Robin Kyle

Ingredients

- 1 box yellow cake mix (I used Duncan Hines)
- 5.1 oz box instant vanilla pudding (the large box)
- 1 cup water
- 1 stick salted butter, melted and cooled slightly
- 4 large eggs, lightly beaten

Filling/Frosting Ingredients

- 1 stick salted butter,
- slightly softened
- 1/4 cup heavy cream
- 1 tsp vanilla
- 7 oz jar marshmallow creme
- 3 ½ cups powdered sugar
- Sprinkles

Directions

1. Preheat oven to 350.
2. Butter and flour 2 (8 inch) round cake pans and set aside.
3. In the bowl of your mixer, combine eggs and butter.
4. Add water, pudding mix, and cake mix and beat on medium for about a minute, until batter is smooth and thick.
5. Spread evenly in prepared pans and bake for about 20-25 mins or until tops spring back when lightly touched, or a toothpick inserted in center of cake comes out clean.

6. Cool cakes for a few minutes in the pans, then turn out on to wire racks to finish cooling.

For frosting/filling:

1. Beat butter and vanilla in your mixer until combined.
2. Add marshmallow cream and beat until smooth.
3. Slowly add powdered sugar until just combined.
4. Add heavy cream, increase speed to high, and beat for one minute, until light, smooth and fluffy.
5. Spread half of filling/frosting on bottom cake layer, then add the second cake layer on top of filling/frosting.
6. Spread the other half of filling/frosting on the top layer of the cake.
7. Add sprinkles on top.
8. Chill for at least 30 minutes and serve.

Rich Potato Chowder

Submitted by Chris Mayer

Ingredients

- 5 to 6 cups potatoes, peeled and cubed
- 1 lb. bacon, cut up before cooking
- 1 to 2 onions depending on size and your taste
- 2 ¼ cups water

Directions

In large stockpot fry bacon until crisp – DO NOT DRAIN
Sauté onion, THEN pour off drippings
Add to pot:
The potatoes and water
1 tsp. salt
½ tsp. paprika OR pepper, whichever you prefer
Bring to boil, cover and simmer 20 – 25 minutes, until potatoes are tender

Mix together:

2 cups sour cream
2 cans cream of chicken soup
3 ½ cups milk
Gradually stir into potatoes until blended
Bring to serving temperature over low heat, do not let it boil again

BOOKS BY TONYA
SOUTHERN HOSPITALITY WITH A SMIDGEN OF HOMICIDE

Camper & Criminals Cozy Mystery Series

All is good in the camper-hood until a dead body shows up in the woods.

BEACHES, BUNGALOWS, AND BURGLARIES
DESERTS, DRIVING, & DERELICTS
FORESTS, FISHING, & FORGERY
CHRISTMAS, CRIMINALS, AND CAMPERS
MOTORHOMES, MAPS, & MURDER
CANYONS, CARAVANS, & CADAVERS
HITCHES, HIDEOUTS, & HOMICIDES
ASSAILANTS, ASPHALT & ALIBIS
VALLEYS, VEHICLES & VICTIMS
SUNSETS, SABBATICAL AND SCANDAL
TENTS, TRAILS AND TURMOIL
KICKBACKS, KAYAKS, AND KIDNAPPING
GEAR, GRILLS & GUNS
EGGNOG, EXTORTION, AND EVERGREEN
ROPES, RIDDLES, & ROBBERIES
PADDLERS, PROMISES & POISON
INSECTS, IVY, & INVESTIGATIONS
OUTDOORS, OARS, & OATH
WILDLIFE, WARRANTS, & WEAPONS
BLOSSOMS, BBQ, & BLACKMAIL
LANTERNS, LAKES, & LARCENY
JACKETS, JACK-O-LANTERN, & JUSTICE
SANTA, SUNRISES, & SUSPICIONS
VISTAS, VICES, & VALENTINES
ADVENTURE, ABDUCTION, & ARREST

RANGERS, RVS, & REVENGE
CAMPFIRES, COURAGE & CONVICTS
TRAPPING, TURKEY & THANKSGIVING
GIFTS, GLAMPING & GLOCKS
ZONING, ZEALOTS, & ZIPLINES
HAMMOCKS, HANDGUNS, & HEARSAY
QUESTIONS, QUARRELS, & QUANDARY
WITNESS, WOODS, & WEDDING
ELVES, EVERGREENS, & EVIDENCE
MOONLIGHT, MARSHMALLOWS, & MANSLAUGHTER
BONFIRE, BACKPACKS, & BRAWLS

Killer Coffee Cozy Mystery Series

Welcome to the Bean Hive Coffee Shop where the gossip is just as hot as the coffee.

SCENE OF THE GRIND
MOCHA AND MURDER
FRESHLY GROUND MURDER
COLD BLOODED BREW
DECAFFEINATED SCANDAL
A KILLER LATTE
HOLIDAY ROAST MORTEM
DEAD TO THE LAST DROP
A CHARMING BLEND NOVELLA (CROSSOVER WITH MAGICAL CURES MYSTERY)
FROTHY FOUL PLAY
SPOONFUL OF MURDER
BARISTA BUMP-OFF
CAPPUCCINO CRIMINAL
MACCHIATO MURDER
POUR-OVER PREDICAMENT
ICE COFFEE CORRUPTION

Holiday Cozy Mystery Series

CELEBRATE GOOD CRIMES!

FOUR LEAF FELONY
MOTHER'S DAY MURDER
A HALLOWEEN HOMICIDE
NEW YEAR NUISANCE
CHOCOLATE BUNNY BETRAYAL
FOURTH OF JULY FORGERY
SANTA CLAUSE SURPRISE
APRIL FOOL'S ALIBI

Kenni Lowry Mystery Series

Mysteries so delicious it'll make your mouth water and leave you hankerin' for more.

FIXIN' TO DIE
SOUTHERN FRIED
AX TO GRIND
SIX FEET UNDER
DEAD AS A DOORNAIL
TANGLED UP IN TINSEL
DIGGIN' UP DIRT
BLOWIN' UP A MURDER
HEAVENS TO BRIBERY

Magical Cures Mystery Series

Welcome to Whispering Falls where magic and mystery collide.

A CHARMING CRIME
A CHARMING CURE

A CHARMING POTION (novella)
A CHARMING WISH
A CHARMING SPELL
A CHARMING MAGIC
A CHARMING SECRET
A CHARMING CHRISTMAS (novella)
A CHARMING FATALITY
A CHARMING DEATH (novella)
A CHARMING GHOST
A CHARMING HEX
A CHARMING VOODOO
A CHARMING CORPSE
A CHARMING MISFORTUNE
A CHARMING BLEND (CROSSOVER WITH A KILLER COFFEE COZY)
A CHARMING DECEPTION

Mail Carrier Cozy Mystery Series

Welcome to Sugar Creek Gap where more than the mail is being delivered.

STAMPED OUT
ADDRESS FOR MURDER
ALL SHE WROTE
RETURN TO SENDER
FIRST CLASS KILLER
POST MORTEM
DEADLY DELIVERY
RED LETTER SLAY

Maisie Doss Mystery

SLEIGHT OF HAND

BOOKS BY TONYA

TANGLED LIES
GRAVE DECEPTION

About Tonya

Tonya has written over 100 novels, all of which have graced numerous bestseller lists, including the USA Today. *Best known for stories charged with emotion and humor and filled with flawed characters, her novels have garnered reader praise and glowing critical reviews. She lives with her husband and a very spoiled rescue cat named Ro. Tonya grew up in the small southern Kentucky town of Nicholasville. Now that her four boys are grown men, Tonya writes full-time in her camper she calls her SHAMPER (she-camper).*

Learn more about her be sure to check out her website tonyakappes.com. Find her on Facebook, Twitter, BookBub, and Instagram

Sign up to receive her newsletter, where you'll get free books, exclusive bonus content, and news of her releases and sales.

If you liked this book, please take a few minutes to leave a review now! Authors (Tonya included) really appreciate this, and it helps draw more readers to books they might like. Thanks!

This book is a work of fiction. The characters, incidents, and dialogue are drawn from the author's imagination and are not to be construed as real. Any resemblance to actual events or persons, living or dead, is entirely coincidental. *Cover artist: Mariah Sinclair: The Cover Vault. Editor Red Adept.*

Made in the USA
Coppell, TX
19 July 2024